©Noboru Kannatuki

GOBLIN SLAYER

3

D1211434

—I wonder how I
look to them?

She enjoyed the passing thought.

If anything, it was Cow Girl
who drew all the attention.

An elegant young woman was
holding hands with an adventurer
in a grimy helmet and armor.

©Noboru Kannatuki

The gold vanished, and
the pair sank into shadows.
Then, a light.

Finally, too
many to count.

Rippling through the
silence of the night...

...a bell
echoed.

—*Riiing.*

©Noboru Kannatuki

Contents

GOBLIN SLAYER

❖ VOLUME 3 ❖

KUMO KAGYU

Illustration by
NOBORU KANNATUKI

YEN ON

NEW YORK

GOBLIN SLAYER

KUMO KAGYU

Translation by Kevin Steinbach ✢ Cover art by Noboru Kannatuki

GOBLIN SLAYER vol. 3
Copyright © 2016 Kumo Kagyu
Illustrations copyright © 2016 Noboru Kannatuki
All rights reserved.
Original Japanese edition published in 2016 by SB Creative Corp.
This English edition is published by arrangement with SB Creative Corp., Tokyo, in care of Tuttle-Mori Agency, Inc., Tokyo.

English translation © 2017 by Yen Press, LLC

Yen On
1290 Avenue of the Americas
New York, NY 10104

Visit us at yenpress.com ✢ facebook.com/yenpress ✢ twitter.com/yenpress
yenpress.tumblr.com ✢ instagram.com/yenpress

First Yen On Edition: August 2017

Yen On is an imprint of Yen Press, LLC.
The Yen On name and logo are trademarks of Yen Press, LLC.

The publisher is not responsible for websites (or their content) that are not owned by the publisher.

Library of Congress Cataloging-in-Publication Data
Names: Kagyū, Kumo, author. | Kannatuki, Noboru, illustrator.
Title: Goblin slayer / Kumo Kagyu ; illustration by Noboru Kannatuki.
Other titles: Goburin sureiyā. English
Description: New York, NY : Yen On, 2016–
Identifiers: LCCN 2016033529 | ISBN 9780316501590 (v. 1 : paperback) |
    ISBN 9780316553223 (v. 2 : paperback) | ISBN 9780316553230 (v. 3 : paperback)
Subjects: LCSH: Goblins—Fiction. | GSAFD: Fantasy fiction.
Classification: LCC PL872.5.A367 G6313 2016 | DDC 895.63/6—dc23
LC record available at https://lccn.loc.gov/2016033529

ISBNs: 978-0-316-55323-0 (paperback)
        978-0-316-55326-1 (ebook)

10 9 8 7 6 5

LSC-C

Printed in the United States of America

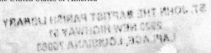

GOBLIN SLAYER

GOBLIN SLAYER

✝

CHARACTER PROFILES

"I am to goblins what goblins are to us."

GOBLIN SLAYER

A strange adventurer active on the frontier. He is famous for reaching Silver (3rd) rank hunting only goblins.

"Protect, heal, save."
—The Three Holy Tenets of the Earth Mother

PRIESTESS

Works with Goblin Slayer. A sweet young woman who must put up with her partner's antics.

"Ignorance is bliss, for learning is the highest joy." —Elven proverb

HIGH ELF ARCHER

An elf girl who adventures with Goblin Slayer. A Ranger and a skilled archer.

The only things that matter to her are the weather, the animals, the crops...and him.

COW GIRL

A girl who works on the farm where Goblin Slayer lives. The two are old friends.

"How can you go adventuring without pen and paper?"

GUILD GIRL

A girl who works at the Adventurers Guild. Goblin Slayer's preference for goblin slaying always helps her out.

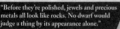

"Before they're polished, jewels and precious metals all look like rocks. No dwarf would judge a thing by its appearance alone."

DWARF SHAMAN

A dwarf spellcaster who adventures with Goblin Slayer.

"A Naga does not run."

LIZARD PRIEST

A lizardman priest who adventures with Goblin Slayer.

"Only a tangled skein awaits those who carelessly spin tales about love or the universe's mysteries...not to mention a woman's beauty."

WITCH

A Silver-ranked adventurer at the frontier town's Adventurers Guild.

"I won't make friends tomorrow with an enemy I respect. I'll do it today."

SPEARMAN

A Silver-ranked adventurer at the frontier town's Adventurers Guild.

GOBLIN SLAYER

HE DOES NOT LET ANYONE ROLL THE DICE.

Life's a roll of the dice
Roll them day after day
And it's always snake eyes
Someone said   luck is fair
Nothing changes til the day you die
Laugh or cry, it's all the same
Snake eyes come up again today
Oh   snake eyes   snake eyes!
Show me a duodecuple tomorrow!

CHAPTER 1

Harvest Moon

A lone wisp of smoke trailed into a pallid sky.

One could trace it back down to find its source, a small hilltop farm.

Specifically, a small, brick building on the fringes of the farm.

Smoke billowed from the chimney into the air like an upward brushstroke.

A young woman stood at the stove in the little building, blowing mightily as she wiped sweat from her brow.

Her skin had the healthy glow of a person raised in the sun. She was plump in all the places a girl should be—but she was not soft.

"Hmm... About like this?"

Cow Girl wiped soot from her cheeks with the cloth draped across the shoulder of her work apron and squinted contentedly.

Her bright eyes were fixed on some pork hung neatly inside the shed, visible through the window.

The smoke enveloped it, gradually bringing out the fat along with an irresistible aroma.

Smoked bacon.

Every year they took pigs that had grown fat on acorns and daisies and smoked them like this.

There was plenty of pork in the little building, and they would let it smoke all day. They would keep up the process for several days—bacon was a labor-intensive product.

So usually, *he* would lend a hand around this time, even if he did it silently.

"Well, I guess when you have work, you have work," Cow Girl said to herself, then laughed as if this didn't bother her one bit.

She knew him, after all. He would come home safely, no question about it, and then he'd help like he always did.

This belief came so naturally to her she almost didn't have to think about it.

"Hup!"

It felt good to stretch as she rose, after crouching so long to watch the fire.

She stood, arms outstretched, ample chest bouncing, cracking her joints and letting out one more great breath.

As she raised her face, a corona of light danced over the dark forest huddled on the horizon.

Dawn. The sun. The start of a new day—although in fact, her day had already been well under way.

Beyond the hill, the wheat fields that ran along either side of the road caught the sun's rays and sparkled. The wind bent the crops gently, creating ripples in a sea of gold. The rustle of the stalks sounded not unlike the ocean.

Or so Cow Girl imagined, anyway. She had never been to the seaside.

Soon the farm's roosters noticed the morning's approach and began to crow.

Their calls coaxed townspeople from their slumber, and thin streams of smoke appeared on the horizon. There were quite a few for such an early hour.

The morning light revealed just how vibrant and lively the town was.

Banners waved atop buildings, streamers in the shapes of dragons or gods whipping in the gust.

The same wind made its way over to Cow Girl, brushing her cheeks as it passed.

"Wow…" She trembled a little at the chill.

The air felt good against her sweaty skin, but it was less cool and more uncomfortably cold.

The sun striving to rise past the horizon radiated with a soft light.

It was fall.

The harvest season had come. Summer was over, and it was time to prepare for winter.

Farm and town had both grown busy.

Lively and prosperous, it was one of the world's beautiful seasons.

Though to Cow Girl, the world was always beautiful.

She knew everyone was working hard—including him.

Yet she also knew he would come and help her. And when he did—yes!

"I'll make him some stew with our fresh bacon!"

First, she would have to make sure he was full and rested.

Just the thought lightened her heart, and she all but skipped on her way back to the main house.

After all, fall was also the time for the festival.

§

The fifth goblin fell around noon.

A stone whistled through the air and caught him in the eye socket, crushing bone and finally striking the brain.

The goblin crumpled where he stood with a thump.

The sun shone on a tunnel entrance resembling a massacre.

".........Hmph."

A warrior watched vigilantly from the shadows of some nearby rocks.

He wore grimy leather armor and a cheap-looking steel helmet. At his hip dangled a sword of a strange length, and a small shield was on his arm.

This shabby-looking warrior was Goblin Slayer.

All he had done so far was subdue the guards, and he was already up to five goblins.

That was not to say, however, that he had hurt his opponents very much.

It had been more than two weeks since the goblins had taken over the mine, which was this village's only source of resources.

Who knew how many more might be hiding beyond the jaws of this tunnel entrance?

Some local women had been kidnapped. It hadn't been long enough for any potential offspring to provide reinforcements. But hostages meant fewer options were open to him. And because the villagers would need to use this mine in the future, ploys involving poison gas or flooding were no good, either.

Presumably, the remainder number fewer than ten. As he considered, his hands nimbly set another stone in his sling.

He stood by a pile of excavated earth, where there was no fear of running out of ammunition.

With close attention to the battlefield, it was possible to use a sling for an entire fight.

"Wh-what do you think, Goblin Slayer, sir?"

Beside him stood a youthful maiden tightly grasping a sounding staff with both hands.

She was slight and willowy, dressed in plain but pure white vestments. It was Priestess.

Goblin Slayer answered without looking at her.

"By 'what,' you mean…?"

"I mean, um, how does it look to you? What do we do?"

"I don't know yet."

As he spoke, he slung another missile through the air.

"GOORB?!"

It split another goblin's skull, one that had ventured out to investigate the guard bodies.

"Six."

The goblin fell prone and rolled into the tunnel. Goblin Slayer counted off softly.

It was simple, drawing like to like.

Not that goblins "liked" each other in any meaningful sense. Most likely the one that had come out had simply drawn the short straw and been forced to go look.

But the principle was the same: use dead or wounded foes as bait to draw out other enemies, then kill them.

That was how he'd reached six total kills so far. He reloaded his sling in a businesslike manner.

"But in any case, this is a problem."

"Meaning…?"

"They have equipment."

"……Oh."

Now that he'd mentioned it, she could see it, too.

Crude though they may have been, the dead goblins all wore armor and carried weapons.

A sword, a pickax, a club, a hand spear, a dagger. Some of goblin construction, some simply stolen.

"Didn't they say three young women had been kidnapped?" Priestess asked, unease clear on her face. "We have to hurry…" Still, she made no move to rush in herself.

It had been more than six months since she'd become an adventurer.

More than six months since she had narrowly escaped death on that first quest. Months in which she had gone on to face death in battle many times.

She was still just Obsidian, the ninth rank, but in many ways she was no longer an amateur. When she heard goblins had kidnapped some village women, she no longer panicked.

Or perhaps she had simply grown numb…?

Anxiety, born of her ever-growing experience, spread through her small chest.

All the more reason she closed her eyes and clung to her staff, praying to the all-compassionate Earth Mother. She prayed the dead goblins would reach postmortem bliss, and that the captured women would be safely rescued.

"It took too long for the request to reach us… Hey." Goblin Slayer waited quietly for her to finish her prayers, then spoke up. "Can you search their corpses?"

"Huh?" She raised her head in surprise, but her eyes met only his expressionless helmet.

"I want to collect their equipment."

"Oh, um…" Priestess wasn't able to answer immediately, glancing back and forth between corpses and the helm.

Of course, it was not that she was afraid, or that the bodies were impure. Goblins or no, corpses were still corpses.

She wouldn't condemn whatever action he chose to take—but could she, a member of the clergy, desecrate those bodies?

"If you can't do it, then back me up."

"Oh, yes, sir." Priestess nodded. "If possible, I'd rather..."

Goblin Slayer made no sound of acknowledgment, but immediately set off running.

Still in the same spot, Priestess heaved a sigh. She kept thinking she was used to this, but somehow she never was.

Sweat beaded on her forehead despite the increasingly chilly wind. She was incredibly alert. She wished their usual companions were with them—especially the elf.

While they were all technically a party, they didn't always adventure together. That was how things had turned out today. Still...

"*Sigh...*"

Priestess found herself letting out yet another groan.

She had too many things to think about, too many things to do.

But Goblin Slayer is still fixated on goblins...

Discussing things wouldn't always be fruitful, of course, but with him you could hardly even get that far.

"O-oops, need to concentrate...!"

She came back to herself suddenly, giving a quick shake of her head. This was no time to be getting distracted.

She held her staff under her arm, preparing her sling. She took a deep breath.

"Are... Are you all right?"

"Yes."

The faint but firm answer drifted back to her.

Goblin Slayer approached the corpses with his usual agile yet unconcerned gait.

"Hmm... Just as I thought," he murmured. "But there's no time to look around here."

He had no use for their armor or helmets. He looted a sword, scabbard and all, from one goblin's hip, drew another's dagger, and collected the pickax from a third.

Pilfered equipment in hand, he headed straight back the way he had come.

"GORB! GRROOORB!!"

"Goblin Slayer, sir! They're here...!"

Goblin Slayer drove on while Priestess fumblingly fired a rock from her sling.

Immediately behind him, a goblin and its reeking breath scrambled out of the mine entrance.

The adventurers weren't the only ones who could use the goblins as bait. The surviving monsters probably thought they had used their companions' bodies to draw the human out.

But Priestess's stone hit the goblin on the shoulder, and he let out a great screech.

"Good."

Far be it from Goblin Slayer to let such an opportunity go to waste.

With a speed belied by his full armor, he flung something over his shoulder with his right hand.

It was the sword from his waist.

"GBBR?!"

It pierced the throat of the goblin with a dull *thock*. Goblin Slayer hadn't even turned around to throw it. The sword he'd stolen was already in his hand by the time the creature's back hit the cavern floor.

"Seven. Others?"

Goblin Slayer dove among the shadows of the rocks, tossing his prizes onto the ground.

"As far as I can see," Priestess said, surveying the entrance to the tunnel, "none."

"All right."

He quickly focused on sorting through the stolen weapons.

He attached the empty scabbard to his belt, using it to resheathe the sword he held. The dagger, too, went by his waist.

Treating the goblins as an armory was his classic strategy.

"We're moving."

"What? Moving?"

Now re-equipped, Goblin Slayer stood.

Priestess, still crouching, blinked up at him in bewilderment.

"I thought this mine only had one entrance."

"It did. Until two weeks ago." Goblin Slayer hefted the pickax and thrust it out at her.

"Eek!"

The casual motion was easy to mistake for an attack.

Priestess glared reproachfully at the helmet.

"Goblin Slayer, sir! B-be careful with that!"

"Look."

"What am I looking at…?"

Puzzled, she obediently leaned toward the pickax, studying it intently.

It was well used, old and dirty, probably left in the mine. Its edges had been dulled from relentless use. They bore dark crimson stains… and particles of earth.

"…?"

Priestess probed the soil with her white fingertip. It was still moist— brand-new.

"Goblin Slayer, sir, does this mean…?"

"Yes."

Goblin Slayer nodded and rested the pickax on his shoulder.

He was well aware that goblins had no knowledge of metallurgy.

They didn't dig holes to find resources—at least, not yet.

This could mean only one thing.

"I would dig a side tunnel and plan a sneak attack."

§

He turned out to be exactly right.

Goblin Slayer set off to the formerly undisturbed side of the mountain.

But now, they found a new tunnel there—along with goblins, crawling out of the hole like worms.

All of them were filthy with mud, tired, and clearly weary… In other words, a perfect opportunity.

"GUAAUA?!"

"Eight."

Goblin Slayer calmly flung the pickax, claiming his next life. The tool may have been blunted, but it was still sharp enough to shatter the creature's sternum and pierce its heart.

At the sight of their fallen companion, the other goblins started a terrible racket.

And who could blame them? This was to be expected.

These fellows had gone on raids in what was their equivalent of nighttime, and then they had been forced to dig this ambush tunnel.

They were unable to sleep, lousy with fatigue, and the higher-ranking goblins were cracking the whip behind them. They had been told their reward would be a young priestess girl—but they figured by the time their turn came around, they would not find her much different from any other prisoner. Naturally, all this sapped their morale.

Goblin Slayer preferred "twilight," but "midnight" would work, too.

Otherwise, what was the point of this tactic?

He quickly took stock of the goblins, thrown into confusion by his ambush.

"One spear, one pickax, two clubs, no bows, no spell-casters."

And just two adventurers.

"Let's go," he said.

"Y-yes, sir!"

Nodding, Priestess followed him as best she could.

He had never and would never be so foolish as to throw away the initiative he gained through a sneak attack.

Goblin Slayer flew like an arrow at the foe while Priestess's staff was raised high.

"O Earth Mother, abounding in mercy, by the power of the land grant safety to we who are weak!"

An invisible field gave him additional protection beyond his shield, repelling the spears of the goblins finally collecting themselves.

This was the miracle of Protection.

"GRRORG?!"

"Nine... Ten."

Goblin Slayer had never stopped moving.

His sword flashed as he eliminated the hand spear goblin, then sliced open the pickax owner's throat.

Priestess coordinated with Goblin Slayer without so much as a word between them.

This was the result of half a year together. Gripping her staff in one hand, she readied her sling with the other.

"GOORB?!"

The spear split in half against the force field, and the goblin, now weaponless, soon found a sword in its skull.

Goblin Slayer didn't so much as spare a glance as the creature collapsed, its brains staining the blade, but with a kick he flipped the pickax up into his hand.

He didn't like two-handed weapons, but at least his shield was strapped to his arm. He wouldn't have any trouble swinging.

"Next."

Goblins were feeble monsters, the weakest of the weak—nothing to fear.

They boasted the size and cruel intelligence of children, perhaps the most common monster in the entire world.

Yes...indeed.

Fighting a few of them outdoors, Goblin Slayer could see where someone might believe that reputation. It was no wonder that many a village tough tried their hand at adventuring after chasing a few of the little creatures out of their village.

A goblin came at him with an awkward swipe of its club, and Goblin Slayer caught both its arms, then its heart, with his pickax.

Filthy blood hissed from the wound.

"GOOROROROGB?!"

"Eleven."

He didn't even bother to spend time pulling the pick back out. He simply let it drop with the corpse.

As he turned toward the last goblin, a stone whizzed past.

"Hi...yah!"

"GBBOR?!"

The goblin yelped stupidly as the rock collided into its cheek with a dull thump.

The creature slumped down. Goblin Slayer jumped on it without hesitation and thrust his dagger into its heart.

"Twelve."

He gave a violent twist of the blade to be sure, then held down the goblin until it stopped twitching.

Finally, he exhaled.

Whatever advantages one might have, there was no time to relax when outnumbered.

But at last, there was a lull.

"Um, Goblin Slayer, sir?" Priestess pattered up to him, fishing in her bag for a waterskin. "Want something to drink?"

"I do."

"Here you go."

He casually took the leather bag, made from a farm animal's stomach. He removed the cap and chugged through his open visor.

Their long acquaintance had led Priestess to fill the skin with a dilute grape wine.

"You have to make sure you get enough to drink."

"True."

As far as she could tell, he was maintaining a good physical condition—in his own way. Still, it only seemed to be the absolute minimum.

I guess it would be strange to say I'm trying to take care of him...

Though she certainly believed he was someone worth taking care of.

Glug, glug. As he drank, she thought to herself.

"That was a good shot," he muttered.

She didn't immediately grasp what the comment meant and gave him a puzzled look. But she soon realized he was talking about her sling.

"Oh... I've been practicing."

She made a fist near her little chest and nodded firmly.

Not that she took any pride in learning deadly arts. But in a certain sense, she was doing it to help people—so perhaps it could be considered one of her trials.

If she were completely helpless in the face of danger, she would only be a burden to her companions. She had begun learning the sling simply to protect herself, but the weapon had proved remarkably versatile.

Goblin Slayer finished his single-minded drinking and replaced the cap.

"Good job."

...Oh!

He tossed the words off casually, but they made her heart swell.

Her cheeks, her whole face, were suddenly hot.

He...just praised me, didn't he?

She could hardly ask him to repeat it, as unusual as it was.

But Goblin Slayer kept talking as though nothing strange had happened.

"We've seriously reduced their numbers. There are probably just two or three left, including the hob."

"A… A hob…?"

Priestess's voice weakened, not pleased with this scenario.

"We haven't seen any totems," Goblin Slayer said with an easy nod, calmly holding out the waterskin to her. "Here, drink."

"Huh? Oh…"

Priestess accepted it with a certain hesitancy. She touched her lips thoughtfully with a slim, pale index finger.

"R-right…"

Goblin Slayer ignored her reluctance to put her lips to the waterskin. Instead he used the tattered rags of a nearby goblin to wipe the fat from his dagger, then returned it to his hip. Next was his sword, still buried in its victim.

He braced against the corpse and extracted the blade, checking the edge and cleaning off the grime before sheathing it.

He confirmed his pack's contents, the state of his equipment, and finally nodded.

"Are you ready?"

"Oh—yes, sir."

"Then we're going in."

A hobgoblin. Two bodyguards. Fifteen monsters altogether.

What became of them was not hard to imagine.

Amazingly, there was some small light to be found among such darkness—all the women were safe.

But how should they go about finding happiness again after being violated by goblins?

Priestess could not imagine.

§

"He doesn't use enough words! At all! Ever!" High Elf Archer pounded the table with her mug. "*I see. Is that right? That's right. Goblins, goblins, goblins*— That's it!"

Her ears bounced up and down, mirroring her sloshing cup of wine.

Her face, normally almost translucent, was bright red while her eyes began to roll.

It was an unbecoming state for a high elf—that is to say, she was drunk.

Night had fallen. Though located in a frontier town, the tavern at the Adventurers Guild was well attended.

Most of the customers had either just finished a job or were preparing to go out on one, and passionate shouts to eulogize the fallen or hearten the wounded punctuated the din.

Given all this, High Elf Archer and the angry steam rising from her ears hardly merited attention. But whether the mood of the bar and her inebriation went well together was another question.

Spearman—by then a familiar face—took a swig of ale from his huge mug and said, "You're upset about this now? How long have you known him?"

"When I ask him if he has plans, I don't really care if he says, 'Goblins.'" She wasn't bothered. High Elf Archer nodded to someone—though nobody was actually there. "He's Orcbolg, right? I'm happy to overlook that. But!" She pounded her mug again, sloshing the wine to leave a red stain on her chest. "That is *not* the answer I expect when I ask for a little help!"

"In other words," Spearman said, dragging a bowl of nuts away from High Elf Archer, "he dumped you."

"He did not!"

She slammed her mug down, though this time she put her whole body into it and heaved a veritable tidal wave of wine from the cup. Spearman ducked to avoid the flying froth.

High Elf Archer pursed her lips and made a sound of displeasure, perhaps regretting the waste.

"That's the problem with you humans. You're so good at making everything about one thing!"

"But he did turn you down for your little adventure, didn't he, lass?"

"Quiet, dwarf!"

She swung the cup at him. But thanks to his minimal height, she connected with only air.

Perhaps because her aim was bad, despite being both an elf and an archer—or perhaps because she was roaring drunk.

Dwarf Shaman was as red-faced as always. Stroking his white beard, he said with immense seriousness, "If y'ask me, I'd say you ought to be offering him help."

"If I'm always doing that, he'll start thinking I *want* to help him."

"And don't you?"

"No!"

She sat sulkily and muttered to herself.

"Goblin this, goblin that. Get your clothes dirty! Don't look at my items! Every single time…"

Dwarf Shaman merely shook his head at the tantrum.

"Never seen someone get so drunk on a single cup of wine. At least she's easy on the coin purse."

"Is it not best to relax from time to time?"

The last remark came from Lizard Priest, who was happily taking bites out of an entire round of cheese. The sight robbed him of the gravitas that usually accompanied a lizard clergyman.

"Nectar! Sweet nectar! If all the world had a bed and a meal as fine as this, there would be no more wars."

"That and wine, perhaps. And then we would fight over what to eat with it."

"Nothing is ever easy in the material world."

Lizard Priest seemed to mull over his words, his eyes wandering the tavern.

"For once, milord Goblin Slayer has gone alone with our dear priestess. Perhaps some feel threatened by this."

"There are, many, rivals, yes?" said a voluptuous woman elegantly savoring her wine—Witch wore a faint wisp of a smile.

She filched a bit of food from Spearman's plate while her eyes turned meaningfully to her neighbor.

"I'm sure I don't know what you're talking about," Guild Girl said with a chuckle.

She was still in her uniform, though her workday was over. Perhaps she had simply stopped by the tavern before heading home. Her cheeks were flushed from drink.

"My, how…easygoing."

"No, not exactly." Guild Girl played with the cup in her hands, hoping to distract them a little. As she spun it gently, miniature waves lapped up in the wine. "I'm just…waiting for my chance."

"Waiting…for five years, no?"

There was nothing Guild Girl could say. She just took a sip from her cup with an unreadable expression.

When she had been assigned to the Guild branch in this town, he was one of the adventurers placed in her charge.

How could she help but notice him as he quietly went about doing what needed to be done?

She saw him off when he left, then waited for his return. There was nothing dramatic about it, to be sure, but—

People's feelings and affections built up in this kind of day-to-day as well.

Though in that sense, I can understand this man's approach, too.

She glanced at Spearman, who Witch interrupted every time he tried to say something. Even Guild Girl could tell he was clearly trying to hit on her.

He was rather handsome, outgoing, and kind to women. The one flaw in the diamond was his tendency to flirt.

He was intelligent, strong, kindhearted, and cheerful. He made good money, and while he could be rough around the edges, he was never unbearable. Objectively speaking, he seemed like a decent man. Guild Girl didn't specifically dislike Spearman. Barring the times when he used to make fun of Goblin Slayer.

But, well, she didn't fall in love with every halfway decent man she saw. Nor was she obliged to respond in kind simply because someone else had become infatuated with her.

"Hmm."

But perhaps, she thought, this made her a rival in love.

It is often said that the friendship of women is fickle, but Guild Girl wasn't so sure.

Spearman's party member, Witch, sat without her characteristic hat but with an inscrutable smile.

"It, is most, demanding."

"For both of us."

The two women exchanged wry smiles, then amicably nodded at each other. The man didn't seem to notice.

"It seems like there have been an awful lot of demon-related quests lately, given that the Demon God was supposed to have been defeated." Spearman took a swig of his ale, perhaps finally brought to heel by Witch. "What's going on?"

Maybe she could talk to him about this. Guild Girl felt a little bad for him, and adventuring was a safe topic.

"My superiors seem to think maybe our heroes missed some of the bad guys."

"I guess just doing in the enemy higher-ups doesn't mean everyone can come right back home." Spearman grabbed a nut and popped it into his mouth, chewing noisily. "Demons are bad news."

"They can disguise themselves as humans, among their other stratagems. They do not make for easy work." Lizard Priest nodded deeply at Spearman, putting his palms together in a strange gesture. "I was most grateful for your help in this instance."

"Don't mention it! There was a quest out, and I took it." He waved away Lizard Priest's gratitude. "And when your adventure doubles as a date, that ain't bad, either."

As Lizard Priest had said, this time the five of them had dealt with a demon in human form.

The quest itself had been terribly mundane: investigate a new cult that had spread through a town.

The small town still boasted a temple of the Supreme God—but it seemed they had lost their sacred implement. The quest involved getting it back. When the question of whether goblins were involved came up, however, the answer was a firm *no*.

It was not a goblin-slaying quest.

"I will go goblin slaying, then," said Goblin Slayer, and Priestess followed after him with a *"Sorry"* and a bow of her head.

"Fine, we'll handle it ourselves!" High Elf Archer had exclaimed, but even she knew they would be less prepared for combat without him.

Just as they were deciding how to address this issue, Spearman called out to them.

It was perfect. The five of them formed a temporary party and set about their investigation…

Naturally, they found ample evidence of kidnappings, drug running, theft, and extortion.

By the time they found the stolen implement, a blue diamond cut to look like an eye, they knew full well what was going on.

Finding the cult's headquarters, where they practiced their bizarre rituals, and capturing their leader was only a matter of time.

"UUUUUU…! AKAATERRRAAAABBBBB!!!"

In the light of the diamond, the cult's second-in-command revealed himself to be the real ringleader—a demon. Of course.

And finally, the demon shed its disguise and engaged the adventurers in an epic battle.

"As you'll recall, it was my arrows that struck the final blow."

"Yes, we know. It's all clearly written in the report." Guild Girl noted High Elf Archer's testimony in her paperwork.

Now the markswoman was dramatically illustrating the battle with wild gestures.

Guild Girl never tired of watching her. The elf was easily 2,000 years older than her, yet felt like a little sister.

"Maybe you've had enough…"

"It's okay. I'm fine! It's just one cup of grape wine. Easy peasy!"

High Elf Archer was completely soused and clearly not "fine."

Well, everyone needs to experience a good hangover once in their lives. Guild Girl wore a dry smile and resolved to help the elf get upstairs once the alcohol wore off, then took another glassful herself. She tilted it back delicately, enjoying the sensation of the wine on her tongue. She thought back to Witch's words from a few minutes earlier.

Many rivals.

Compared to the priestess, who could go with him on adventures, it was true that Guild Girl was at a disadvantage because all she could do was wait.

What disadvantage? Don't be silly.

Around here, even a receptionist could take the offensive.

Yet somehow, she was a tiny bit scared of taking that step…

She was surprised how much she enjoyed their relationship as Guild employee and adventurer. But if it were to stop there…?

Out of the corner of her eye, she saw Witch chiding Spearman as he tried to call, "Are you troubled, miss?"

Guild Girl found herself breathing a small sigh. And at that moment…

"___?"

The swinging door to the building creaked open.

Then came the sound of casual, indiscreet footsteps.

High Elf Archer's ears perked up, like a hunter catching the sound of a rabbit.

Then they saw him: an adventurer in ridiculously second-rate equipment. Equipment so pathetic it caused a stir even among the Porcelain ranks—the complete beginners. An adventurer whose unique outfit was known to one and all at the Guild.

Goblin Slayer.

"I'll take care of the paperwork. You rest."

The blunt instruction was directed at the priestess following behind him.

She hardly seemed able to bear her fatigue. Her head bobbed up and down, eyelids half closed.

A priest's spells were called miracles because, exactly as the name implied, the caster made a direct supplication to the gods in heaven. The effort this demanded was no less than a frontline warrior's, and it had taken a serious toll on this willowy young woman.

"…Yeess, sir… Um…"

"What?"

"G'd night… Goblin Slayer, sir…"

She nodded heavily at Goblin Slayer's words and weaved her way up the stairs.

He waited for her to safely reach the second floor on her unsteady feet before setting off.

But the others could hardly just watch him walk up to the front desk.

"Hey, Orcbolg, over here!" High Elf Archer called out at the top of her lungs after she recognized her distinctive companion through the haze of alcohol. She stood up and waved her wine cup madly at him, splashing its contents into Spearman's snack.

He wearily chewed on a wine-soaked nut, earning Witch's giggle.

Goblin Slayer came over to the table and took in the scene.

"What is it?"

Dwarf Shaman and Lizard Priest shared a glance and shrugged.

They weren't sure whether or not they found it comforting that Goblin Slayer was exactly the same immediately after an adventure as he was at any other time.

"You know perfectly well what!" High Elf Archer, however, did not seem pleased. She smacked the table repeatedly and glared up at the steel helmet. "When you get back from an adventure, you ought to at least say hello!"

"Is that so?"

"It is!"

High Elf Archer snorted. Guild Girl smiled at her, then slid aside. She gestured Goblin Slayer to sit down, which he obligingly did. She turned her smile to him and said, "Welcome back, Mr. Goblin Slayer. How did it go?"

"I will make my report," he said, then cocked his head. "Is your shift not over?"

"Oh, come on," Guild Girl said, pursing her lips with a touch of annoyance. "I'm always the first to hear about your adventures. Why not tell me?"

"Hm." Goblin Slayer folded his arms and thought. Then he declared, "There were goblins."

"Wow, who could have guessed?" Spearman growled. He shrugged his shoulders and shook his head as if to say, *This guy doesn't get it.* "What our dear Guild Girl is asking is, does what you did stack up against what we did?"

Goblin Slayer lapsed into thought again.

"We slaughtered fifteen of them."

Spearman knew better than to expect some detailed anecdote about Goblin Slayer's adventure, but even he hung his head in disappointment.

"Come on, Goblin Slayer. Throw us a bone, here!"

Witch squinted absentmindedly and put her glass to her lips.

"Perhaps, there's no bone, to throw..."

"When Beard-cutter's been about, I suppose there wouldn't be."

"We do speak of milord Goblin Slayer. He has his quirks."

"They had equipment."

Dwarf Shaman and Lizard Priest nodded knowingly at each other, but Goblin Slayer shook his head.

"The kidnapped women were all safe."

"Really?" Guild Girl blinked. "That's wonderful, but...quite unusual."

She had been working here for five years, and she rarely heard of such a thing.

Though she lacked actual experience adventuring, she had heard more about it than anyone else. Certainly more to do with goblins. Sometimes the information came before the women were kidnapped, sometimes immediately after. Sometimes two weeks after.

"Were they being kept for food...? Or did someone in command want them as hostages?"

"No." He shook his head. "They were injured, and terrified."

"This was in a mine, wasn't it?"

"Targeting a mine was strange enough."

"Meaning they weren't after food. Hmm..."

Guild Girl demonstrated how she was among the few who could follow Goblin Slayer's conversation. She tapped a finger against her lips as she digested the bits of information he shared.

She hardly even noticed Spearman exclaiming, "Maybe I should just study up on goblins, then!"

In cases involving goblins, the creatures would abduct young women eight or nine times out of ten. But this was largely to use them as sexual slaves, playthings to vent their anger.

The same way most people found goblins repugnant, goblins couldn't abide humans.

Guild Girl knew many examples of brutality that, as a fellow woman, made her wish she had neither heard nor read about them.

One might have expected her to be thrilled at hearing news of the rescue.

"…Hmm. So we really don't know enough to say anything yet…"

Something seemed to bother Guild Girl. She tilted her head, trying to grasp what it was.

Maybe it was the same for Goblin Slayer. He said dispassionately:

"That's my preliminary report. I'll file a more detailed one later. Have a look at it."

"Sure. Of course, my shift is over for today, so it'll be first thing tomorrow morning…"

"That's fine."

"Not by me, it isn't!" High Elf Archer broke in.

Laid out on the table, she glared up at Goblin Slayer, struggling to make her heated glare appropriately threatening.

"…Who cares about your dumb report? You should greet your friends and companions first! …I know goblins are more important to you, though," she muttered.

The armored man slowly shook his head.

"You already know I'm here. There's no need."

"It doesn't matter. You should do it anyway."

"Is that how it is?"

"…Everyone was worried about you."

This provoked a murmured "…Were they?" from Goblin Slayer. "I will change."

"That's good." High Elf Archer's face melted into a mellow smile, finally content.

Her ears flicked with her bettered mood.

She swore that by the time they reached 2,000 years old an elf was considered an adult, but she certainly didn't act it. *Frankly, she might be something of an embarrassment to her high elf ancestors.*

At least, that's what Dwarf Shaman was thinking when Guild Girl moved quietly.

She leaned nonchalantly and put her hand on Goblin Slayer's knee.

The motion was strikingly natural, and she appeared completely serious.

"By the way, Mr. Goblin Slayer."

"What?"

"The, um, the harvest festival is the day after next."

"Yes."

Guild Girl breathed in and out with a soft sigh. She put her hand to her chest, as if trying to physically restrain her pounding heart.

"Do you...have any plans?"

The atmosphere changed instantly.

Even the adventurers chattering and drinking nearby stopped to listen, never mind the people at their table.

She felt her nerves tighten the way they did upon entering a dungeon.

Witch used Silence to prevent Spearman from exclaiming, "I'm free!"

High Elf Archer's eyes were open, but her inebriation allowed her to offer only a sluggish, incoherent murmur.

And at the center of that indescribable mood, Goblin Slayer spoke.

"...Goblins."

"Ah, I mean...any *non*-goblin plans?"

".......Hm."

With that single sound, Goblin Slayer lowered his head as if lost in thought.

Or perhaps at a loss for words. Either would have been an unusual sight.

As everyone around them waited with bated breath, only Guild Girl still had a smile on her face.

After a moment, Goblin Slayer said, "...No, I suppose not."

"You know, I'm taking off the whole afternoon that day."

She seemed to be waiting for some kind of response.

It's now or never!

It was festival season, and she had been planning for this moment. He had just finished a goblin-slaying quest, and the reward for her unstinting hard work allowed her to take time off when it really mattered.

There was also the wine. Borrowing strength from the alcohol, she figured this would be her best chance.

"I... I thought m-maybe you'd like to go...see the festival with me."

"..."

"I—I mean, the festival...it might not be completely safe, right...?"

One of her fingers drew meaningless shapes in her palm. Guild Girl watched the steel helmet.

That same cheap thing he always wore hid the face behind it.

The only way she could reach him was to keep talking, though her voice was increasingly strained thanks to her racing heart.

To Guild Girl, every second he was silent felt like—a minute? No, an hour.

"…All right."

Goblin Slayer nodded.

His voice might have been dispassionate, almost mechanical, but there was no mistaking what he said.

"You are always a great help to me."

"Ah, right—I— Thank you," she said with a bow, flinging her braid into the air.

Whoops. Do you say "thank you" in this situation?

She was a bit concerned, but it was a small thing, completely overwhelmed by the joy spreading quickly through her heart.

"Ah—oh, right! Mr. Goblin Slayer, would you like something to eat?"

"No, I'm fine." With a firm shake of his head, Goblin Slayer rose from the bench. As always, he checked his armor, weapons, shield, and gloves with a practiced eye, then nodded.

"Once I make my report, I'll go back for the day."

"O-oh, I… I see." Guild Girl felt a strange mix of emotions, disappointed but also pleased with this very characteristic answer.

"In that case, um…"

"The day of the harvest festival, at noon, in the square. Will that do?"

"Yes!"

"All right, then."

Goblin Slayer nodded, then surveyed everyone at the table.

"What will all of you do?"

Guild Girl managed to keep her head out of her hands, but her face clearly betrayed her sentiments. She should have seen this coming.

Lizard Priest and Dwarf Shaman felt the same way. They merely shrugged and decided to do what they could to help.

"It is my intention to spend that day enjoying a meal with Master Spell Caster."

"Ah, yes! I've always wanted to drink Scaly under the table once. This will be a good chance."

Dwarf Shaman pounded himself on the belly, then rubbed High Elf Archer's back.

"Come with us, Long-Ears. No matter what they say, elves and dwarves belong together!"

"Bwah?" A noise of disagreement left her mouth. It was the sort of formless sound a child made to protest getting out of bed.

"Ah, come now—I'll treat you to a cup of wine!"

"…Okay."

"I see." Goblin Slayer accepted their answer with his usual coolness, then made to leave.

Spearman opened his mouth as if to say something, but Witch interrupted. "The two of us have a date."

"I'll be going, then."

Not so much as a word of farewell. As always.

He headed for the front desk and flagged down the nearest employee to make his report, then went outside.

His bold stride contained no hint of hesitation, as always.

He was a somewhat strange adventurer.

The group watched him go, unable to say anything.

"Gracious me," Lizard Priest said, letting out an admiring breath. "A most impressive strike."

"Heh… Ah-ha-ha… I'm just glad it went well." Guild Girl blushed shyly and played with her braid.

"Indeed." Witch smiled, giving ashen-faced Spearman a little pat. "You, tried hard, too."

Dwarf Shaman let out an exasperated breath. "Anvil-chest here could learn a thing or two from you."

"Aw, shut yer yap." High Elf Archer turned, slowly and cumbersomely, to glare at the dwarf. "I just want to go on an adventure together. That moron won't even come with me!"

"Yes, lass, you've failed quite miserably."

"Wa…Waaaah!"

"Ah, come now. Here, have a drink."

He poured a copious amount of wine into her cup. She spared him a quick glare before putting the cup to her mouth with a little nod.

Guild Girl, watching all this, knitted her brow apologetically.

"Um, I... I'm sorry..."

"Pfft. Like I care. I told you, I don't think of him that way." High Elf Archer took dainty sips of her drink, watching Guild Girl. "Hey," she said.

"Yes?"

"That was a good line: 'Any *non*-goblin plans?' Can I use it?"

§

When Goblin Slayer left the Guild, a sweet aroma enveloped him.

Now what could this scent be...?

Even as he was wondering, a gust of cool breeze carried the smell away.

As the sun set, the day's warmth receded as though it had never been.

The night approached. He stared up at a cold sky dotted with stars.

The twin moons, full with the promise of a rich harvest, gleamed with a light that was somehow metallic, inorganic.

"Hm."

It was autumn already.

But it meant very little to him.

After the harvest, goblin raids on villages would probably increase.

There was a style of fighting appropriate for spring—as well as one for summer, for winter, and, yes, for autumn.

He scanned the silent streets.

The banners and streamers hanging in anticipation of the festival, along with the wooden towers, cast a complex network of shadows on the ground. Goblin Slayer weaved between them as he walked.

These were streets he knew well, but each time he passed a shadow, he reflexively made a fist.

Perhaps there was nothing skulking in the darkness. But goblins could appear at any time and any place.

Not all preparations were helpful, but one could never be too prepared.

This was one of Goblin Slayer's most cherished principles.

"Oh, there you are!"

Thus he could take the unexpected, but familiar, voice in stride.

The bright, friendly greeting didn't quite match the night—though perhaps he needed the light.

"Oh," Goblin Slayer said. "You came to meet me?"

It was, of course, Cow Girl.

"Heh-heh!" With a smile on her face and a bounce in her chest, she pattered quickly toward him. "I wish I could say I did. I just happened to be in town. Work, you know."

"Is that so?"

"Yeah, it is." She nodded firmly. The grimy helmet followed her intently.

"A delivery?"

"Uh-uh." Cow Girl shook her head. "Talking to a client. Uncle told me to handle it so I would learn about the business side of things."

"Is that so?" he said again, nodding.

The sun was absent and the town dark, leaving the two alone in the blackness. The street outside the town gate was even more lonely and dark.

"...Shall we go home?"

"Yeah, let's."

They set off, falling into step beside each other.

They followed their own shadows stretching out along the flagstones and silently headed home.

Not in a hurry, but not taking their time.

The lack of conversation didn't bother them. Sometimes it was quite nice.

"Ah..."

With a whoosh, the cool wind blew again and brought that pleasant fragrance with it.

Goblin Slayer couldn't quite seem to remember what it reminded him of.

A single flower petal danced through the air, accompanying the breeze and smell.

Goblin Slayer looked up. He saw a tree blanketed in golden flowers.

"Oh, it's fragrant olive." Cow Girl followed his gaze upward and used her hand to shield her eyes from the brightness of the leaves. "It's blooming already. I guess this is the season."

It had been a flower's aroma.

"So it is," murmured Goblin Slayer, now that he knew where the odor was coming from.

It was strange how the frame of pale yellow flowers made even the cold moons seem warm.

As he started walking away, he suddenly felt a soft sensation surround his left hand.

Cow Girl had clasped his gloved hand in hers.

She was blushing just enough to be visible, her eyes averted ever so slightly.

"I mean… It could be dangerous, to walk while you're looking up like that. It's… It's dark."

"…"

"I'm sorry. Did I…?"

She glanced at his face, trying to decide how to take his silence.

After a moment Goblin Slayer, his expression hidden by his helmet, slowly shook his head.

"No."

"Hee-hee."

And Cow Girl set off, pulling Goblin Slayer behind her.

He could feel her warmth through his armor. Holding on to that sensation, he trailed behind her.

She glanced at him out of the corner of her eye.

"By the way…"

"What?"

"Do you know what the fragrant olive symbolizes in flower language?"

"Flower language?" Goblin Slayer repeated, as if he'd never heard the expression before. "No, I don't."

"Well, I think you should find out, then."

She sounded very much like a child trying to emulate an adult.

Cow Girl chuckled and smiled knowingly, wagging her index finger slightly.

"To me, I think it suits you."

"…I'll keep it in mind."

Goblin Slayer nodded, and Cow Girl responded in kind with a "Mm" of affirmation.

Should I bring it up?

Cow Girl had managed to break the ice.

Despite his helmet, he wasn't that hard to read. Still, he could be surprisingly stubborn, so she would have to use her head.

"…The festival's coming up—it's already the day after tomorrow."

"Yes, it is." He nodded assiduously. "I was invited to it, myself."

"Gwah?!" A strange cry escaped her.

"What's wrong?"

"No, I—uh, I mean— Who invited you? And what did you say?"

"The receptionist from the Guild. I believe you know her."

Cow Girl nodded.

Guild Girl. Stylish, capable, and thoughtful. A mature young woman.

"I had no reason to turn her down. I asked everyone else if they wanted to come along, but it seems they all have plans."

Cow Girl suddenly stopped walking.

"…What's wrong?"

"Ah… Ahh-ha-ha-ha-ha-ha!"

With her free hand she played with her hair to distract him.

Gah. She beat me to it…

Whether or not he understood what she was thinking, Goblin Slayer repeated dispassionately, "What?"

"…Aww, it's nothing." Cow Girl shook her head slowly.

It's… It's not that big a deal. Is it?

So she hadn't gotten what she wanted.

She wasn't sure she ought to give voice to her thought now, but it was only words, right?

"I just… I was hoping to see the festival with you, too. That's all."

"Were you?"

"Yeah."

She nodded, then they fell silent again.

Before they knew it, the flagstones had given way to a dirt road, and they walked out through the great main gate.

In the spring, this hill filled with daisies. It was where the adventurers had done battle with the goblins. Now, with winter approaching, all that remained was the grazing grass and their own crunching footsteps.

When he listened closely, he could hear the faint *liii, liii* of some insect, and his old friend's breathing beside him.

It had grown colder, but not so much that their breath fogged.

"...Hey."

"What?"

"What time's your date?"

"Noon."

The farm's twinkling lights were appearing in the distance.

Goblin Slayer kept his eyes—his helmet, rather—forward as he answered quietly.

"Oh," Cow Girl whispered, drawing her trembling hand to her chest. "Then... Could I ask for your morning?"

"Yes."

"Wha?"

She had been about to retract such a forward request, and now all she could do was stare.

The grimy helmet blended with the darkness so well she could barely tell where the steel ended and the night began.

Just like how she couldn't quite tell whether he was being truthful.

He was easy enough to understand, but—wasn't she projecting her own desires onto his words?

Cow Girl gulped. She wished her voice wouldn't shake.

"R-really?"

"Why should I lie?"

There was no hitch in his voice.

Of course he wasn't the kind of man to tell such a foolish lie. She knew that.

"But it's... You're sure...?"

"That is not the question." He dismissed her anxious inquiry easily. "You asked me to."

"Oh... Then...if you're okay with it?"

"I don't mind."

"Hooray!"

Cow Girl could hardly be blamed for her excited whoop after his matter-of-fact response.

She jumped in the air, her generous chest bouncing, and spun around in front of him.

"All right, it's a date! The morning of the festival."

"Yes." Overwhelmed, Goblin Slayer cocked his head in puzzlement. "Does it make you that happy?"

"What a question!"

Cow Girl reminded him of what he should have already known with a huge smile.

"It's been almost ten years since I went to a festival with you!"

"Has it?"

"Sure has."

"...I see." Goblin Slayer shook his head with the utmost seriousness. "I didn't realize."

They could just barely catch the scent of boiling cream. Cow Girl had left the dairy cooking when she thought it was about ready, *going to meet him* under the pretext of an errand.

Now the house was right in front of them.

Of a Surprisingly Troublesome Woman

Oh, heavens.

It's wonderful to see you sleeping well and showing a healthy glow of late.

But I do wish you'd act a little more grown-up.

Your bedding is all messed up…

How old are you? It's unbecoming.

Oh, don't pout.

You are hopeless…!

Isn't revered archbishop a very important position?

You can't just drop by a festival anytime you like.

And there's so much to do—cleaning up after the incident with the Evil Sect, solving those riddles…

What in the world were those explosions near town recently? Two of them, no less!

All that noise, how distracting… What is this world coming to?

This is why we so dearly need the power of the Supreme God. Act grown-up, for our sakes.

All right, wash your face, comb your hair, put your makeup on. Make yourself presentable.

Some very important guests are coming today, and we must look our best.

That man whose help you requested recently was certainly devoted to his work, wasn't he?

It's so important to be dedicated to our duties…

…Ah, there's that grown-up look.

Hee-hee. Ahh, yes, this is good.

If you have something on your mind, perhaps you could send a letter. I'll gladly pen one down for you.

Here, fragrant traditional paper and brand-new ink.

Yes, yes, that's the spirit. A little fun makes us all the more ready to work.

Now, our guests today are… Well, there are three of them.

You know the ritual taking place during the festival?

It seems they hope you'll write them a recommendation letter to view the ritual of the Earth Mother.

…Oh, no! I said, don't pout! You'll ruin your makeup…

Gracious me! And to think, this is the famous Sword Maiden!

Noboru Kannatuki

CHAPTER 2

FESTIVAL'S EVE

Goblin Slayer's day started early.

He woke before daybreak, donned his equipment, and patrolled the farm.

The predawn hours made for good night vision practice.

Particularly once summer was over and fall had begun, the mornings became dark and cold. A time well suited to him—and to goblins.

In those chilly minutes before the horizon became visible in the distance, he devoted himself to training and vigilance.

Eyes on the ground ahead, weapon in hand, he took one careful step at a time.

If a goblin appeared at that very moment, he would have calmly and quietly dealt with it.

That was how thorough he was—how thorough he wanted to be.

"Morning! It's a little nippy today, huh?"

Once the sun came up, his old friend rose to the crowing of roosters.

She complained about the temperature, largely because she wore nothing but her underwear and a bedsheet.

She leaned out the window, happily exposing her ample bosom. It was no wonder she was freezing.

"You'll catch a cold." Goblin Slayer hardly looked at her, dispassionately sheathing his naked sword.

"Aw, I'm used to it. I'll be fine. Breakfast will be ready in a few, okay?"

"No…" He cocked his head as if listening for something, seemingly thinking to himself. Finally, he slowly shook his head. "There's something I have to do first."

"Oh, really?"

"Please, go ahead and eat. And…" He considered for a moment, but when he spoke, it was in the same tone as always. "I will probably be late tonight."

"…Sure. Okay." Cow Girl pursed her lips with a touch of disappointment, but soon she was smiling again. "Be sure to put away your utensils when you're done eating."

"I will."

With a wave, she disappeared from the window. He turned away from her, his gaze settling on the barn.

Well, really just the unused storehouse he happened to be renting.

He opened the door with a creak and went in.

The floor was cluttered with unidentifiable equipment and items. He shoved things to one side or the other to make space.

He sat down in the open area he had haphazardly created, removed the sword from his hip, and took out a whetstone.

In the thin light, Goblin Slayer could see that the blade was starting to warp, chipped and rusting.

It was often said that a single sword could not cut down more than five people before it dulled with blood and fat. It was true.

But how many times did a world-class chef, standing in the kitchen all day, whet his knife?

For an outstanding swordsman, to kill a hundred people was essentially the same thing. For what was a sword, really, but a knife for cutting meat?

In the heat of battle, it was a different story. Doubly so for crude swords stolen from goblins.

To him, weapons and armor were consumables. They could be taken from the enemy if need be.

"…"

But that was no reason to neglect the care of one's equipment.

Goblin Slayer started polishing his sword.

He scoured off the rust, beat the blade straight again, and used the whetstone to grind flat the chipped places.

In general, people believed that a sword that could bend without breaking was a good piece.

But the only thing good about this weapon was the skill of the Guild manufacturer who made it. It was clearly a simple work of mass production, not some famous blade. The way it was, he could throw it away without hesitation.

"Next."

He put the sword back in its scabbard and moved on to the next piece of equipment.

For better or for worse, he had entirely replaced his shield, armor, and helmet during the events in the water town. He didn't particularly mean to use them forever, but he was grateful for them, all the same.

As a result, all they needed was a gentle polish and a quick inspection. His boots demanded considerably more attention, though.

They, too, were nothing special, the kind that could be found anywhere. That being said, they were important for walking and running through caves and across plains, kicking and crushing enemies. He could hardly stand being mired in normal tracts of mud, let alone a Snare trap.

He checked the treads of the boots, scraping off any encrusted earth and polishing them.

He checked the laces, and if they were fraying, he replaced them with new ones.

This alone reduced the chance of taking an unfortunate stumble—and that was reason enough to do it.

Next were his socks. Their importance could not be underestimated. They were crucial for preventing blisters and foot problems on long treks over bad terrain or through swamps.

His master had had little use for footwear, but that was because his master had been a rhea. The small-statured race normally went barefoot, which was to say that their own limbs were the best "shoes."

If you could go anywhere without making a sound, without ever slipping, you had nothing to fear. Goblin Slayer had always thought this was a skill worth learning.

"Now."

Having given his equipment a once-over, he stood slowly.

A helmet with dark crimson stains seemed to have fallen from a shelf.

It was a piece of old equipment. Goblin Slayer picked it up and put it back in its place.

Now his store of items was nicely arranged. It was time to get some farm equipment, too.

Letting the whetstone lie where it was, he was about to leave the shed when he saw a figure in the doorway.

"…You're a hard worker."

"…Yes, sir."

He caught the barest wisp of tobacco smoke in the crisp morning air.

The farm's owner was leaning against the wall, puffing on his pipe.

He wore a somber expression, and Goblin Slayer bowed his helmet ever so slightly.

"Good morning, sir."

"Morning," the owner said with the bluntness of a club. "I hear you promised to go to the festival with my girl."

"Yes, sir."

"…As her adoptive father, I'm not sure if I should be angry about that."

He spoke with a sour look. Their eyes met. But then he smiled.

Goblin Slayer had entirely forgotten what the man's smile looked like, he realized.

The owner scrunched up his face, lowered his head, and scratched at his thinning hair.

"Not to butt into your business, but…," he murmured to no one in particular. "I know you don't mean to lead her on. But, well…don't lead her on."

"Yes, sir."

"I've heard you've got a fair number of women around you... I know, I know. You're not the type to be too affected by that."

"Yes, sir."

"She probably knows that, too... But spare a thought for her feelings once in a while."

"...Yes, sir."

The owner observed Goblin Slayer's firm nod, and that unreadable expression returned to his face.

"As long as you understand. Or..." He cut himself off and cast a dubious glance at the helmet. "*Do* you understand?"

"I believe I do," Goblin Slayer answered. "Though I'm not confident."

At that, the owner rubbed the bridge of his nose with a finger.

"...What do you plan to do, after this?"

"After I finish maintenance on the farm equipment, I thought I might go to town to do some shopping."

"Will you, now...?"

The owner chewed gracelessly on the end of his pipe and closed his eyes. He seemed unsure what to say next.

When he finally spoke, it was in a strained voice.

"...At least wait until after breakfast."

"..."

"That girl made it for you."

"Yes, sir."

"You've got a day off for once. Take it easy."

"Yes, sir. However..." He stopped for a moment, almost lost. "Time off is something I don't understand very well."

Goblin Slayer did not forget to clean up after breakfast.

§

It was underwear.

Or more accurately, it was armor that strongly resembled underwear.

The set included a chest covering, gloves, and a little something for the lower body. Categorically speaking, it might be called light armor.

In terms of mobility, it easily outperformed a full set of plate mail.

The armor itself was beautifully curved, elaborate, and solid.

The problem was it just didn't cover enough surface area.

It was just chest armor—really, *breast armor*—and panties.

There were shoulder pads, true, but that wasn't really the issue. One good hit to the abdomen and an adventurer's innards would be sunning themselves. It provided no defense against a stab to the back, either, a wound that could easily be critical.

Well, in that case, at least the armor provided easy access for the administration of first aid. Or maybe it was supposed to help its wearer focus on not getting hit.

But at the end of the day, was anyone really prepared to wear nothing but this over their bare skin?

Surely it needed a supplement—a chain-mail shirt, some kind of under-armor? It might at least stop a fist.

"No, no, no, that'd never work."

"Why not?"

"Covering yourself up would hide exactly what makes a woman attrac—"

Female Knight stopped and cast a sideways glance at the grimy warrior standing next to her.

"Ugh. Goblin Slayer?!"

"Yes." He nodded.

They were in the equipment shop at the Adventurers Guild.

There were piles of items all around. In the workshop near the back, the master and his apprentice pounded away with their hammers.

Goblin Slayer frequently came to order new items, but this was the first time he had seen Female Knight there. Partly, this was because a knight's equipment—from their beloved plate armor to their swords and shields—did not need replacing often.

How could someone like her, who needed serious protection to survive her role in the vanguard, even consider armor like this?

"Are you planning to switch to light armor?"

"Huh? Me? Oh, no, I just..." Her usual firm manner vanished as she trailed off and stared at Goblin Slayer out of the corner of her eye. "Frankly, seeing you makes me want to give up wearing leather armor."

"Does it?"

Goblin Slayer cocked his head. He was the very picture of *scruffy*.

Chain mail and dingy leather armor, topped by a cheap-looking helmet that hid his face.

Of course, the toughness of wax-treated leather armor was not to be sneered at. It was certainly lighter than metal armor, but if well made, it allowed the wearer to remain agile. Helmets were out of favor with young and up-and-coming adventurers, but they did protect against a sneak attack to the head. In combination with the chain-mail undershirt, it was perfect for fighting goblins in tight, dark spaces.

"Couldn't you, you know—" Female Knight observed him from top to bottom, trying to find the right words. "—polish it a little?"

Maybe just take those mysterious crimson stains off it.

"This is deliberate." Goblin Slayer spoke with the same dispassion as always, yet there was a hint of self-satisfaction at his own knowledge. "It keeps goblins from noticing my scent."

"...At least keep your body clean."

"Yes." Goblin Slayer nodded, grave. "Or people will get angry at me."

Female Knight presumed he was being serious. She raised her eyes to the ceiling as though praying to the gods.

She wasn't looking for an oracle or handout, of course. It was just something she did in the heat of the moment.

I think I'll quit asking questions while I'm ahead.

"...So. What are you buying today?"

"Stakes, and two coils of rope. I also need wire and wood. I must replace my shovel, as well."

"........" Female Knight gave an involuntary groan. "Come again?"

"Stakes, and two coils of rope. I also need wire and wood. I must replace my shovel, as well."

"What kind of adventure do you need all of that for?"

"It's not for an adventure." Goblin Slayer shook his head. "It's for slaying goblins."

Female Knight heaved a sigh. Of course.

But Goblin Slayer was oblivious to her reaction, instead studying the armor with great interest.

It looked to him like a two-piece set of underwear, something he would hesitate to call armor.

"What is this? Piecemeal armor?"

"In a sense, I guess," Female Knight said, but Goblin Slayer didn't really understand what she meant. To all appearances, it was considerably more than "piecemeal armor," but considerably less than "armor." No one in their right mind would wear this on any adventure where they might run into monsters.

Well, maybe certain talented fighters could pull it off. Or perhaps someone in the rear lines—a wizard or thief, or even a monk.

Having come to this conclusion, Goblin Slayer shook his head gently.

"It would never work."

"...It's... Adventuring women, you know..." Female Knight seemed to be trying to answer his objection. But her face was red, and she couldn't quite look at him. She could barely get the words out, very unlike her usual self. "I mean, there aren't...a lot of interested guys out there."

"Is that so?"

Goblin Slayer tilted his head.

Female Knight, at least, struck him as quite pretty.

Her lovely golden hair. Her almond eyes. She had beautiful facial features, too, and her skin seemed smooth. If she put on a dress, she could pass for a noble's daughter.

But she only answered, "Yeah, it is." And so it must have been.

"Think about it. Guy adventurers always end up marrying princesses, or some village girl they rescued."

"So I hear. I cannot speak from experience." Goblin Slayer inclined his helmet slightly.

He recalled hearing such stories from books when he was a little boy.

The knight slew the dragon and rescued the princess. He took her back to his castle, where he refused the kingship and instead traveled far away.

And in a far, strange land, he married the princess and founded a new country.

"Well, take my word on it."

Goblin Slayer had the same serious tone he used when solving riddles. "So? What about it?"

"Well, what do you think happens to all the leftover female adventurers?" Female Knight's expression was despondent and grim.

"Hm," Goblin Slayer muttered, crossing his arms. "Perhaps they could marry one of their companions."

"I know plenty of parties that broke up when love got in the way and the situation got to be unbearable."

"Terrible tales."

Indeed. Goblin Slayer spoke of the topic with great gravity.

He had seen more than a few parties with many women in them, but keeping them together was a task.

Although, he had also heard that parties of only women often got along quite well. He seemed to recall hearing some such thing from an Amazon once upon a time.

He hadn't figured it would be of any particular benefit in goblin slaying at the time, but on reflection he wished he had asked for details. After all, he now had two women in his party. So the stories hadn't been as irrelevant to him as he'd thought.

"Then find a husband who is not an adventurer."

Anyway, right now he had to talk to the person he was with. Goblin Slayer offered what he thought was a practical suggestion.

But Female Knight gave him a smile with despair fit for the end of the world.

"You really think any guys are out there waiting for a girl who can take down a troll or a dragon with one swipe of her blade?"

"Aren't there?"

"...Well, what would *you* think of a woman like that?"

"That she must be quite reliable."

"...Never mind," she said, giving Goblin Slayer a dubious look and a deep sigh. "Personally, I don't really have any interest in non-adventurers, but..." The normally implacable knight shuffled from one foot to the other, unsure where to rest her gaze. "...Maybe it would pay to seem just a bit less...tough."

"Yes." At this point, Goblin Slayer finally began to put the pieces together.

That thickly armored fighter in her party—Heavy Warrior.

Goblin Slayer pictured the chiseled face of a man always taking care of the youngest members of their group.

"Is it him?"

"...Yeah."

Female Knight answered with the slightest nod, the picture of an innocent girl.

Wait...

Goblin Slayer let out half a breath.

He had always taken her to be older, because of her measured demeanor, but perhaps she was younger than he'd realized.

Well, so it went.

"I thought love among party members made things unbearable."

"There's exceptions to every rule!"

"I see."

"...Hey, uh, Goblin Slayer... It kind of kills me to ask you this, but..." Female Knight gulped, and this seemed to embarrass her afresh as she flushed red. "If I... If I wear something like that, do you think it'd get his attention...?"

"I confess I must doubt the sanity of anyone who would ask me that question."

"Urg..."

Standing in front of the bikini armor, Female Knight found herself at a loss.

As an unwavering wall in combat, she wasn't used to taking a critical hit.

"If you want to launch a surprise attack, you need to change it up."

"...Huh?"

It would have been a discredit to her role as a tank if the unexpected statement was enough to stun her, though. She doubtfully shifted her stance.

"Trying similar things again and again will have little effect. At least, in goblin slaying."

"...I'm not asking about goblin slaying."

Female Knight glared at him in exasperation.

Goblin Slayer crossed his arms. He thought, then he continued dispassionately.

©Noboru Kannatuki

He really had nothing to draw on but his own experience.

"You're talking about clothes. You normally wear armor. So get away from that. Wear civilian clothes."

"Er... C-civilian clothes...? ...O-okay. I'll think about it."

"I see."

"Yeah. Um...sorry for the strange question."

"I don't mind." Goblin Slayer shook his head. "We're colleagues."

That caused Female Knight to blink.

She wasn't ready for that, it seemed. She stared intently at the grimy helmet, and then her face relaxed.

"...You're a strange, stubborn weirdo."

"I see."

"But it turns out, you're not a bad guy."

That was her surprise attack. She smiled.

"See you," she said brightly, and left Goblin Slayer standing there, speechless.

§

"Keh-heh-heh! How about that? I think she likes you."

Goblin Slayer found the papery laugh's source, the master of the workshop.

How long had he been listening? The old man, short enough to be mistaken for a dwarf, came out into the shop.

Goblin Slayer moved his recent exchange to the back of his mind, striding boldly up.

"I want to make an order. Stakes and—"

"Think I couldn't hear you? I've got it all ready here. You, boy, bring out the goods!"

"Yessir!"

The apprentice quickly obeyed his master. He carried stakes, wire, and all to the counter.

"Thank you," Goblin Slayer said, and began to inspect the items.

Some items had to be ordered at this workshop, but others they already had in stock from somewhere or other.

Now with everything he needed, he tucked the items under his arm.

He propped the shovel against his shoulder, then hung everything else from it in a bundle.

Adventurers quickly learned how to pack everything into the smallest possible space.

"You done a pretty good job making yourself popular here over the last five years, haven't you?"

Goblin Slayer pulled his purse out of his pack, letting some coins clatter onto the counter.

The master counted them out with a beefy finger, sliding them across the flat surface. His eyes narrowed in his wrinkled cheeks.

"Have I?"

"Y'have."

"I see."

"Yep."

The old man smirked, as if recalling an embarrassing bit of history about a relative.

"When you came in here, some fifteen-year-old kid who wanted cheap equipment, I figured I'd never see you again."

"As the most cost-effective approach, it was the appropriate choice at the time."

"True, and I thought you might upgrade one day. But you kept wearing those items out and getting new ones."

"Would it kill you to buy a decent sword every once in a while?"

Goblin Slayer didn't reply.

He knew this was all the equipment he needed for slaying goblins.

Even if there had existed an enchanted sword just for killing goblins, this adventurer probably wouldn't have used it.

"Ah, well." The master leaned against the counter like an old man tired of his own foolishness. "In the mood to buy anything else today? I've got something just a tad unusual."

"What?"

"A Southern-style throwing knife."

"Oh-ho."

Goblin Slayer's reaction didn't escape the master's notice.

"Got your attention, have I?" the old man said with a bold smile. He didn't wait for an answer before he turned around.

He took a strangely shaped knife from a shelf and set it on the counter with a solid *thunk*.

It was a most unusual dagger.

The blade split outward into three stems, each bent like a branch. It didn't seem intended for typical hand-to-hand combat. The only way to use it would be to throw it.

But it was clearly a knife—in other words, not a very formidable weapon.

"Little invention of mine. What do y'think?"

Goblin Slayer took the twisted weapon in his hand. He took a stance, made a few casual swipes, and finally nodded.

"Goblins would have trouble imitating it."

"Anyone would have trouble imitating it!"

"…What are its advantages?"

The master frowned. But despite his taut features, he went on happily, perhaps enjoying the opportunity to discuss his weapon.

"I know what it looks like, but it's really a sword."

His finger, rough from years of working the forge, pointed to the three blades.

"It spins when you throw it—for stability, and to make it go farther. It's more for cutting than stabbing."

"So are Eastern throwing knives."

"Those are piercing weapons. *Low-quality* piercing weapons."

"I see."

Goblin Slayer ran his finger along the windmill-like blades.

It looked passable, at any rate. It couldn't hurt.

"I'll take one, then."

"Pleasure doing business. Five…no, four gold coins."

A bit expensive for a throwing weapon, but Goblin Slayer counted it out readily.

He lined the brand-new coins up on the counter, and the old man took them without even pausing to ensure their quality.

This young man, this single-minded goblin hunter, much preferred weapons like this to any legendary armaments.

He had been a regular customer here for five years, and any shopkeeper who couldn't figure out a customer's preferences after that long would quickly be out of business.

And he very much doubted this unusual man was the type to try to pay with counterfeit currency.

"And scrolls. If you get any in, set them aside for me." Goblin Slayer hung the fan-bladed knife behind him, from his belt. He tried drawing it several times, moving it around until it no longer bumped up against his item pack.

The shopkeeper watched him with a satisfied expression and replied easily, "Sure, just like always. Don't see too many of those, though. Anything else?"

"Hmm."

Finally satisfied with the throwing weapon's placement, something suddenly seemed to occur to Goblin Slayer.

"…I wouldn't mind some dried fish."

"I sell armor and weapons here. I'm not a fishmonger."

"I see."

The expressionless helmet tilted. The shopkeeper sighed.

All these strange requests. Does he really understand…?

"…If preserved is all right…I've got some."

"In that case, please deliver two or three barrels of them to the farm."

"Barrels? I told you, this ain't the grocers."

But it came out as a mutter. The old man took out his order book, licked his pen, and wrote it down.

§

Finished with his shopping, Goblin Slayer left the armory with his usual unconcerned stride.

He marched boldly to the Guild's bulletin board, studying each new quest.

All the other adventurers had chosen their quests already. The bulletin board was visible in places where pieces of paper had been removed.

Dragon problem. Unexplored ruins. Ogre (what was that?). Gathering resources in the forest. A treasure hunt. A vampire in an old castle (he'd heard of such creatures). Exterminating rats in the sewers. Taking out a band of brigands.

Periodically he saw words like *Evil Sect*, *Dark Gods*, *demon slaying*, and *investigation*.

He searched from the upper right to the upper left, row by row, until he wound up at the lower left.

He repeated this two or three times, then finally reached a conclusion.

"...Nothing today."

This was unusual. Goblins could appear anywhere, at any time.

He glanced toward the front desk, but saw no sign of Guild Girl.

"...Hrm."

With the slightest of grunts, he headed for the desk anyway.

His metal helmet swiveled left and right, until he spotted a Guild employee who seemed to have time to kill.

"Hey."

"Wha—? Uh, ah!"

The startled employee dropped the book she had been secretly reading behind her ledger.

The employee—Inspector—picked up her book like nothing had happened and quickly put on a smile.

"Ah, if it isn't Goblin Slayer."

The eccentric adventurer was famous around the Guild in more ways than one.

"Is this about yesterday's quest? We have the reward ready to pay out..."

"All right, then. Please divide it into two bags. Evenly."

"Certainly, sir."

"I would also like to make my detailed report."

"Ah... You can give it to me, if that's all right..." Inspector hesitantly glanced at a back room of the office. "I hope she won't hold it against me, though..."

Goblin Slayer didn't really understand what Inspector was muttering about.

"You're not assigned to me, so I might not understand everything. Would another day be all right?"

"I don't mind," Goblin Slayer said with an indifferent nod. "But—is she okay?"

"Oh, she's fine." Inspector lowered her voice to a whisper, clearly mindful of her surroundings, and smiled. "There's a lot to take care of before you take time off. She's had to be everywhere at once today."

"I see."

"Can I tell her Goblin Slayer was worried about her?"

"I'm not worried." But he didn't exactly refuse, adding "I don't mind" with a nod.

Inspector's smile broadened. He turned his helmet to indicate the bulletin board.

"Goblins. None today?"

"Goblin slaying? Just a moment, please." Inspector vanished into the back room and returned with a leather pouch from a safe.

She measured out the gold coins inside with a scale, then transferred them to two new bags.

"Here you go."

"Thanks."

"Now, as for goblin slaying…"

Goblin Slayer nonchalantly took the reward and tucked the two bags into his item pouch. While he did so, Inspector took out a register and thumbed through the pages.

"Let's see… You're right. It appears there are no requests involving goblins today."

"Were there any that somebody else already took?"

"No, sir. It doesn't seem so for today."

"I see," Goblin Slayer said with something like a low groan.

"You seem disappointed."

"Yes." Inspector had spoken lightheartedly, but Goblin Slayer nodded seriously. "Very disappointed."

"Sorry I couldn't help," Inspector said, bewildered by his response. Goblin Slayer turned and walked away.

Goblins were thieving, scheming creatures. Though they created crude weapons and tools, it never crossed their minds to make their own food or even their own dwellings. They survived by stealing what they needed…

"..."

...In other words, they were biding their time.

Goblin Slayer grunted and shook his head. He glanced around the lobby as he gathered his thoughts.

"Arrgh! My head feels like it's gonna burst! And Guild Girl isn't even here!"

"Silly. It's because, you drank, too much."

There was Spearman, holding his formerly addled head, and Witch, at it as usual.

"Oh, hey, you're back. Geez, how long does it take to buy one item?" Heavy Warrior said, resting his chin on his hands. Female Knight blushed furiously.

"O-oh, hush. There are all kinds of things I have to consider..."

Half-Elf Fighter jumped in playfully. "Well, even our beloved Knight wants to look stylish for the festival!"

"Wow, really?! Aw, that's great. I wonder if I should wear a dress or something, too," Druid Girl said, cupping her cheeks with her hands. But Scout Boy quipped at her coldly.

"You wanna look stylish, huh, Sis? ...Well, you're beautiful on the inside, at least."

"Wh-what did you say?!"

"Hey, keep it down, don't shout!"

Heavy Warrior's party was quite enamored with discussing the festival. Next to them, Rookie Warrior and Apprentice Priestess affected disinterest.

"Are you just gonna stick to your votive robes? I was kind of hoping to see you in your ritual clothes..."

"Watch it, or I'll lay you out."

"Yeah, but I mean, it's a *festival*..."

"......W-well, I guess *maybe* I could...dress up a little..."

"Really?! Woo!"

"Hey, don't make such a big deal about it, you're embarrassing me!"

The other adventurers were the same way. Everyone brimmed with excitement for the upcoming festivities. Not a single person wasn't looking forward to it.

"...Almost no one," Goblin Slayer murmured within his helmet as his gaze met with an adventurer sitting in the corner. The young man wore a black overcoat, almost defiantly, and watched the adventurers with a glittering gaze.

It wasn't unusual. Ambition was necessary to succeed in this line of work.

Goblin Slayer began to walk slowly, watching everyone in his peripheral vision.

There were always too many things to think about. Always too few clues.

And much to do, he thought...

"Mph."

"Oh!"

Priestess came bustling in from outside and all but ran into him. She straightened herself and clutched her cap.

"Oh, uh, ah, G-Goblin Slayer, sir!" Her cheeks flushed before his eyes, though he had no idea what she was embarrassed about. He almost expected steam from her ears as he cocked his head.

"Were you able to sleep last night?"

"Y-yes. I'm fine."

Maybe he was just being paranoid. Priestess's eyes wandered from one place to another anxiously.

"Mm," Goblin Slayer grunted faintly. "I want to give this to you before I forget."

"Whoa!"

Goblin Slayer passed her the coin purse, and Priestess received it with both hands to keep from dropping it. The bundle jangled quietly as she clutched it to her modest chest.

"From yesterday."

"Th-thank you..."

She put the reward money away carefully, but her thoughts seemed to be elsewhere. Her gaze kept darting to the workshop.

Goblin Slayer was quiet for a moment before asking flatly, "Need new equipment?"

"Oh! Uh..."

He seemed to have guessed right.

Now her whole head turned, swiveling back and forth between Goblin

Slayer and the workshop. He could not fathom what could be bothering her so.

"Do you need advice?"

"N—" Priestess's voice squeaked out of her. "N-no, I...don't. I'm just...fine...thank you!"

"I see."

He left it at that, walking past her.

To him, at least, all this was perfectly natural. The guffaw from the old man behind him didn't even elicit a glance back. Maybe the senior was interested in the girl.

That wasn't—shouldn't have been—a bad thing.

§

They say the time before a festival is its own festival.

When he went out into town, he heard hammers pounding wood, banners flapping, the breeze blowing.

Adventurers weren't the only ones who lived in this frontier town. Young women browsed the stocks of shops, decorated for the celebrations, wondering what to do about their clothes. Children ran along the broad streets, no doubt wondering how to spend their pocket change. It would be all too easy for their plans to unravel at the sight of some toy in a store display...

Strangely cut vegetables were drying by the roadside, awaiting the time when they would be woven into lanterns. More carts and carriages than usual ran through the street.

An abundance of food and clothes were on sale, and visitors were in no short supply, either. It was only natural, with a festival coming.

This area was still the frontier, forever attacked by monsters, threatened by Demon Gods, and under development. Hence, it was understandable that at festival time, at least, everyone wanted to enjoy themselves as much as they could.

"Hmm."

Goblin Slayer cast a glance at all this, then quietly headed down the street behind the Guild building.

The sunlight shone down at an angle, much weaker than in summer. The sun hung high in the sky, but the cool breeze made it feel like a spring day.

The smell of something broiling drifted from the Guild's gallery.

In fact, wisps of cook-fire smoke were rising from many of the houses in town. It was time for lunch.

So that's what those children were running toward.

The training grounds were empty. Any adventurer on a quest would have set off already, and the rest likely weren't so dedicated to their training as to skip lunch.

Perfect.

He dipped his head once and headed to a corner of the grounds, where he sat down in the shade of a tree.

Then he set down his shovel and untied the bundle attached to it, quickly setting up shop.

Stakes, wood, wire, rope, et cetera. A variety of items, many of them unrelated to adventuring.

After drawing his short sword, he started his work immediately.

He shaved down the stakes to incredibly sharp points, pounded them into the wood, and angled them. Then he wrapped the rope around it all in an unusual fashion.

His movements were broad, yet precise, but whatever he was making seemed too dangerous to be for everyday use.

If High Elf Archer had been there, she no doubt would have fluttered her ears in curiosity. Priestess would have hesitatingly asked what he was up to.

But it was neither of them who called out to him as he sat there absorbed in his work.

"Oh!"

"Ho ho!"

Two very intrigued voices. Goblin Slayer raised his helmet briefly.

One man shaped like a barrel, another tall and slim. Dwarf Shaman and Lizard Priest—two of his companions.

Their shadows—one tall, one short—overlapped with that of Goblin Slayer under the tree.

"Ah, milord Goblin Slayer. Another fine day today." Lizard Priest joined his hands in a strange gesture, unapologetic for staring at Goblin

Slayer. "We hope the weather for tomorrow's festival is as congenial as this."

"Yes." Goblin Slayer nodded without pausing in his work. "I hope it will be sunny."

"Agreed, agreed." Lizard Priest slapped the ground with his tail. Next to him, Dwarf Shaman stroked his chin.

"Aren't we the hard worker. What've you got there?"

"I'm setting something up."

Goblin Slayer had few words for the dwarf, who studied the apparatus with his hand still on his beard.

It was something or other involving a number of stakes, a shovel, some wire, and some wood.

Lizard Priest's eyes rolled in his head and sparkled at the prospect of battle.

"Are you planning to drive out a vampire?"

"…?" Goblin Slayer tilted his helmet. "What makes you think that?"

"I believe it is well established that one defeats a vampire with a stake of white wood."

"Is it?"

"I suppose we should be impressed that you even know what a vampire is," Dwarf Shaman said, half exasperated and half amused.

Vampires ranked with dragons as famous monsters of the world.

Of course, greater knowledge of the undead was secret, known in detail only to wizards and clerics. But for a man who didn't even know what an ogre was, being able to recognize vampires deserved special notice.

"I'm not very interested in them."

After his brief and altogether foreseeable answer, Goblin Slayer went back to sharpening the stakes.

But then he murmured, "Hm," and suddenly stopped working, tilting his head. "Vampires… They increase their numbers by biting people, do they not?"

"Or so one hears."

"…If a goblin were to become a vampire, I wonder how I would prepare."

Dwarf Shaman sighed, but Goblin Slayer was completely serious.

"Well, now," Lizard Priest said, touching the tip of his nose with his tongue. "A dead goblin is a goblin corpse. If it were to move, would it not be considered some kind of zombie?"

"Be that as it may," Dwarf Shaman retorted, barely able to restrain his laughter, "I can't imagine anyone wanting to drink goblin blood to begin with."

"I see." Goblin Slayer bobbed his head firmly. Whether he was responding to Lizard Priest's suggestion or to Dwarf Shaman's was not clear.

Then he resumed his work, and the pile of shavings grew as they watched.

Dwarf Shaman brushed away wood chips with his thick fingers, then set to work picking out the ones lodged in his beard.

"This for goblin slaying?"

"It is."

"Thought so."

This was where High Elf Archer usually would have put her ears back with a frosty change in attitude.

But after half a year together, Dwarf Shaman was used to these things. He let it pass.

"S'pose I shouldn't ask the details, then."

"It is impossible to know where goblins will emerge from."

"True indeed," Lizard Priest said, his tail swishing gently. "One must be vigilant at all times."

"Yes." Goblin Slayer nodded. "They're stupid, but they're not fools."

Goblins had no desire to learn—but where they did learn, they could use tools and strategy. Even Dwarf Shaman and his friends had been hard-pressed dealing with goblins that had learned enough to attempt a naval engagement in an earlier adventure. If a strategy spread among the goblins, it meant trouble—but this particular man was very thorough.

Dwarf Shaman and Lizard Priest were both, in their own way, professionals of their races. The dwarf was passionate about smithing and working, while the lizardman had a heart for battle and strength.

To them, obsession and stubbornness had a kind of beauty.

"May we have this spot beside you, then?" Lizard Priest asked courteously.

"I don't mind," Goblin Slayer said impassively. "I do not own this place."

"Aw, still polite to ask," the dwarf said. Even as he spoke, he spread out a large cloth and plopped himself down.

Lizard Priest untied a bundle he had been carrying, spreading its contents on the cloth.

A glance was enough to tell the materials were for some kind of craft, but not necessarily what it would be. He had strips of bamboo, thin pieces of paper in many colors, along with oil paper.

"Mm," muttered Goblin Slayer, not showing the least hint of surprise. "Paper lanterns...no, sky lanterns."

"Ho, you're a sharp one, Beard-cutter," Dwarf Shaman said approvingly as he began assembling the pieces with deft motions.

The strips from the knobby bamboo trees were light and strong, and the sky lanterns formed from them were a classic part of festival scenery.

They were simple enough to make: paper draped over a bamboo frame. Then oiled paper would be set into the frame, and the lantern would be lit.

"And then, so I am told, they float into the sky." Lizard Priest slowly shook his long head, as if hard-pressed to believe it. "This I must see with my own eyes. I am truly looking forward to it."

"They used to make these in my homeland. I'm doing this for Scaly."

"Mm." Goblin Slayer nodded, examining his stake in the light. "Not perfect... But not bad."

"Then my expectations for it are all the higher," Lizard Priest said, swinging his tail in one of his meaningful gestures. "For I place great faith in what you say, Goblin Slayer."

"...Is that so?" was the whole of Goblin Slayer's reply. He set himself to the next stake.

The dwarf understood what it meant when a craftsman lapsed into silence. "Come on, then, we ought to get started, too." He took up the materials with a gentle smile. "Festival's tomorrow. Need to be ready."

"Indeed. I await your instruction."

Lizard Priest coiled his long tail and sat down gently next to Dwarf Shaman.

But the dwarf's hands moved so quickly. Who would have guessed his stubby fingers could do such fine work? He wove one frame after another, his production no less magical than any of his spells.

No one could match the dwarves for handiwork. Even elves were a step behind.

Lizard Priest's job was to place the paper covers over the finished frames. He tried hard to keep his claws from tearing the paper, but frankly, it was quite difficult for him.

At the same time, though, his work was precise and thoughtful. It seemed to reflect his personality.

"I wonder what custom lies behind these things," Lizard Priest said. He exhaled and wiped his brow, as if to clear off sweat that could not be there.

Dwarf Shaman grabbed a wine jug in one hand and wet his lips, then murmured, "Good question. I'm not from these parts, myself. I know how to make a sky lantern, but not why they use them at this festival..."

"...You see them in many places," Goblin Slayer said briefly. The others looked at him, surprised.

He kept paring down the stake, seemingly oblivious to them.

"They attract good spirits, or drive out bad ones. They show the dead the way home. They're similar to vegetable lanterns."

"Know quite a bit about them, eh?"

"My hometown," Goblin Slayer said, "was near this festival. How could I not know it?"

"Mmm. I confess it makes little sense to me." Lizard Priest scratched his nose with a claw.

His people believed dead things returned to the ground, or into the flesh of those who ate them, in a great cycle. The "undead" were not those who had returned from death, but corpses possessed by evil spirits.

"But..." Lizard Priest's eyes rolled in his head. "Mourning the dead, we understand. Perhaps it is good to think they will come home."

"...I agree." Goblin Slayer nodded. "It should be."

Then he said no more. His hands kept working, his expression completely hidden by his helmet.

Each time the shavings piled up, he swept them away, refreshing his blade whenever it dulled on the wood.

Lizard Priest, who had been watching him intently, let out a soft breath.

"In any case, it is a festival. We must do ourselves proud, as much as we can."

"Good for you, Scaly, getting into the spirit."

"But of course. My faith is in my forefathers, the naga, whose blood flows in my veins. They are my ancestor spirits."

His behavior would not bring shame upon his forebears. The dwarf nodded appreciatively. That was something he understood.

"Better not let up, myself. I'll show them the best lanterns any dwarf has ever made!"

The trio of men chatting on the edge of the training grounds was bound to attract notice eventually. As lunch ended, people began coming back to train. Others were hanging around the Guild after finishing their adventures. It was not surprising that some noticed the three.

"Oooh! Shorty and Orcbolg are making something together!"

And if a normal person noticed them, a high elf would notice them twice.

The clear, almost childish voice was of course that of High Elf Archer.

She came running up like the wind and stood with her hands on her hips.

Dwarf Shaman glowered up at her, stroking his beard, and teased, "What are you, a kid?"

"How rude. I am two thousand years old, you know?"

High Elf Archer snorted, but stuck out her flat chest slightly as if proud of this number.

The insult didn't stop her from turning nimbly to look at what they were working on.

"Whatcha makin'?"

"Long-Ears, my friend. Two thousand years and you don't recognize this? It's a sky lantern. It's—"

"It's a stake."

"Not what I meant."

After her comment, the elf slid down onto the cloth by Dwarf Shaman. Lizard Priest heaved himself up and moved aside to make room for her.

Her ears twitched, and her eyes glittered with interest. She fired off questions one after another. "What's this? What's that? What's this tool? What's it for? Why are you making a stake?"

"It's for goblin slaying."

"You don't say."

Her pace was like a whirlwind. They say women travel in herds, but she was noisy enough to be a crowd all by herself.

"You could almost pass for a rhea," Dwarf Shaman said with a touch of reproof.

The lively commotion naturally drew others.

"Hey, isn't that that Goblin Slayer guy and his crew?"

"Oh yeah. Are they getting ready for the festival?"

It was Scout Boy and Druid Girl, along with Rookie Warrior and Apprentice Priestess, back from lunch. They were still scarcely more than boys and girls. Festival preparations still filled them with wonder and anticipation.

Even for Scout Boy, who had been with Heavy Warrior's party for several years, the annual festival was cause for excitement.

"Hey," Scout Boy said, "what's that?!"

"Don't you know?! Those are—"

"Sky lanterns! I've seen them before." Scout Boy thrust out his chest, eager to boast. High Elf Archer, who had lost her chance to explain, puffed out her cheeks.

"How about you join in, then?"

"I am unaccustomed to this, myself. We can learn together."

The dwarf and the lizardman didn't hesitate to invite the children to join them.

High Elf Archer seemed to have no compunction about all of them being there together—almost enough to cast her status as a high elf into doubt.

".........."

Goblin Slayer turned his helmet, taking in the bright, cheerful surroundings. The smiling faces, all laughing with one another, had formed a circle with him—all these adventurers.

At the center of it were the two making lanterns.

Most likely, they all would have gathered like this even if he hadn't been there. And yet...

"Hmm."

Goblin Slayer silently set to work with his knife again.

§

"What?! Orcbolg, you haven't eaten yet?!"

"No."

Night came quickly in autumn. Dusk had come and gone already, the sky an inky black punctuated only by the moons and stars.

Goblin Slayer had stayed while his friends had drifted away bit by bit.

"That won't do... Wait, is it because you don't have the money...?"

"It isn't."

"I'll treat you!"

"Not necessary."

"What if goblins attacked? Could you fight on an empty stomach?"

"...Hrm."

"Okay! It's decided, then!"

High Elf Archer grabbed him without waiting for a response and dragged him to the tavern.

Plenty of people in this frontier town besides adventurers spent time there. It was as good for eating as for drinking. And because most taverns also had guest rooms, it always bustled with travelers.

The tavern High Elf Archer chose at random happened to be such a place with an attached inn.

They pushed open the door with a creak and were greeted with a wave of noise and body heat. Along with the lively chatter of the drinkers packed into the seats came the mingled aromas of wine and meat.

"Mmm!" High Elf Archer narrowed her eyes appreciatively, her ears bouncing.

"I thought you didn't like wine."

"Fair enough," High Elf Archer said with a wink. "But I love an upbeat atmosphere."

"Is that so?"

"It sure is... Oh, two, please!" She cheerfully held up two fingers to the waitress who came out to greet them. Luckily, there were seats available.

The waitress, who was dressed in a provocative outfit and walked with a seductive gait, led them to a round table some ways from the center of the room.

Goblin Slayer set down his pack and sat, the old wooden chair groaning quietly.

High Elf Archer, on the other hand, settled down with the lightness that was the specialty of her people and elicited not a sound from her chair.

"...Hey, I keep thinking," she said, her thin, white finger indicating Goblin Slayer. "Can't you at least take that thing off at mealtimes?"

"I cannot." The helmet moved gently from side to side. "What if goblins attacked?"

"Right here in town?"

"Goblins can appear in town."

She gave a tired, helpless smile.

It was not difficult to understand her perspective. After all, Goblin Slayer's strange appearance did stand out, even among adventurers, with the grimy leather armor, the cheap helmet, the sword of strange length, and the little round buckler fastened to his arm. Luckily, it wasn't unusual around here to see adventurers who kept their equipment on, even in their day-to-day. However...

"What's that...? An adventurer?"

"I thought it was an undead or something..."

"Yikes, it looked at me!"

"So I wasn't just imagining it..."

...this restaurant was not frequented exclusively by adventurers. And the various travelers there had obviously noticed him.

There were only one or two other customers who appeared to be adventurers, sitting in a corner of the tavern where they wouldn't be too conspicuous. One was tall while the other was a diminutive rhea.

He might have been a wizard, judging from the cloak that covered every inch of skin. His appearance was not that unusual among adventurers.

Perhaps discussing a quest, they appeared to be arguing vehemently, though their voices did not carry.

High Elf Archer flicked her ears suspiciously, but eventually lost interest.

"So," she said, turning her gaze from the two adventurers back to the helmet. "What are you going to do?"

"About what?"

"About the festival tomorrow. I heard, you know." A mischievous smile played across her face, and she pointed at him. "You're going to spend the morning playing around with that girl from the farm and the afternoon with Guild Girl, aren't you?"

"I am not playing." His response was utterly brief. He fixed his gaze on her from within his helmet. He might have been glaring at her, but his visor made it impossible to tell. "You have sharp ears."

"Well, I am an elf."

She made a point to twitch the knifelike ears she was so proud of and wore a catlike grin.

"Sounds like she's made plans for your afternoon together, so that's taken care of."

"Hrm."

"I just thought maybe you had something to do in the morning, since you're finally going on a date and all."

"Is that so?"

"It is."

"…Not yet," Goblin Slayer grunted, shaking his head. "I haven't even thought about it yet."

"You're impossible," High Elf Archer said, widening her eyes and kneading her brow as if to relieve a headache. "But at least you're always you, Orcbolg."

Her expression quickly changed to one of interest, her ears flitting up and down. "Anyway, what if you take her someplace she likes?"

"Someplace she likes…?"

"Yeah, or do something she enjoys… You've known her a long time, right?"

This time it was Goblin Slayer's turn to seem perplexed. High Elf Archer nodded with satisfaction.

"Also, you have to say more than just *I see*, *That's right*, *Is that so?*, *Yes*, and *No.*"

"Hrk…"

High Elf Archer ignored the gulping Goblin Slayer, turning her attention to the menu on the wall.

"What to order, what to order?" she said, in a tone that expressed her joy clearly even without the help of her ears bobbing along.

Her purse must have been bulging with the earlier day's reward. Left to her own devices, she would probably have burned through it in a flash.

"Anything you want to eat, Orcbolg?"

"Anything is fine," Goblin Slayer said quietly. "You're paying. Get whatever you like."

"Sheesh. I can't tell if you're trying to be considerate or what."

"It's my nature."

"Yeah, I know."

High Elf Archer sighed, but her annoyance lasted only a moment.

"Excuse me!" She waved to a waitress, then proceeded to request a large swath of the menu. She started with a wild greens salad of some sort, and when she found out there was a top-quality grape wine available, she didn't hesitate to add it. At this point, Goblin Slayer could not help breaking in.

"I will not be able to see you home if you get drunk."

"Erk," she said, her ears trembling as if this were completely unexpected. "I can't believe you think I would get too drunk to walk."

"Wouldn't you?"

"That only happens on very rare occasions!"

She sniffed, but Goblin Slayer continued in a clipped tone, "I have things to do after this."

"*Sigh…*"

She turned her head away as if disinterested.

The servers wove their way through the crowded restaurant like adventurers dodging traps. Her eyes followed the steam rising from the plates they carried, until her gaze found its way back to Goblin Slayer.

"…You need any help?"

"No." Goblin Slayer shook his head, then after a moment's thought, spoke again. "I'm all right for now."

"Hm."

Then they fell silent, making no effort to talk until the food arrived.

To the other customers, the silent adventurers were just one more strange part of the scenery.

The food that finally arrived included soup, bread, and cheese. And wine.

The steaming soup was grain boiled in sweet cream. The hard, black bread could be dipped in the soup to soften it up. The moist cheese was salty and savory for an excellent accompaniment to the soup.

"I bet I know someone who'd like this place." High Elf Archer laughed, prompting an "Indeed" from Goblin Slayer.

"Not that dwarf, though. I'm sure he'd complain about the wine tasting like water or whatever. Guaranteed."

"You mean fire wine?" Goblin Slayer gulped some of the wine through his visor. "It's a good tonic, and a good fuel. Also useful as disinfectant."

"I assume you're not joking. But that stuff is not fit for drinking."

She giggled, her laugh ringing like a bell.

"Orcbolg… That reminds me." She pushed her plate aside, leaning in so her face was close to his. She appeared cheerful, but her voice was strained.

"What?"

"Today… Did you know that girl did some shopping at the workshop?"

"Yes."

"That girl" was likely Priestess.

Goblin Slayer nodded.

"Well, what do you think of the equipment she bought?"

"Hm?" This time, he shook his head. Through the very slight haze of the wine, he pictured her from that afternoon. He poured some water from the carafe into his glass and took another gulp. "I didn't ask."

"Oh, really?"

High Elf Archer blinked, muttering, "Unusual" in surprise as she played with her glass.

"Hmmm. Well, maybe I should keep it to myself, then… You wanna know?"

"If you want to tell me, then I'll listen."

"If the question was whether I wanted to, I'd say I do. But she really didn't say anything to you?"

"No."

"I'll keep her secret, then," High Elf Archer said with a wink. This was not a typical elven gesture. She had picked it up from living in town. She smiled, amused to be borrowing human body language. "I think it'll be more interesting that way."

"Do you?"

"Sure do."

"Do you, now…" Goblin Slayer nodded once more, then searched in his item bag.

He pulled out the leather pouch containing his reward, almost smiling as he reached inside.

"I will pay while you can still remember."

Clack, clack, clack. He lined up three gold coins on the table.

In an instant, the elf's expression changed from relaxed to hostile.

"I said I'd treat you."

"Sometime—"

Goblin Slayer, most unusually, cut himself off. It sounded as if he himself didn't believe what he was about to say.

"…Sometime, I may…ask for your help."

"Paying in advance, huh?"

"Yes."

"Hmm."

We must be drunk.

Her and Orcbolg both.

Well, I guess…huh. It's okay.

"No need."

"…I see."

Goblin Slayer nodded impassively.

High Elf Archer stuck out a pale finger, drawing a lazy circle in the air.

"You can pay me back by going on an adventure!"

"Erk."

"Didn't I tell you already?" the high elf adventurer asked as she took a sip of wine. "Oh, *non*-goblin-related, of course."

"..."

Goblin Slayer was silent. He probably had no idea what to say. High Elf Archer held herself back, waiting to hear what would come out of his mouth. Elves were used to waiting. Ten seconds, ten years—it made no difference.

"All right… Thank you for your help."

"Great!"

Now that she had his promise, High Elf Archer puffed out her cheeks. She narrowed her eyes like a cat and let out that laugh that formed in the back of her throat and emerged like the ring of a bell.

"Now come on, let's eat. It's gonna get cold."

"Right."

As he set to his meal, Goblin Slayer glanced at the corner of the tavern. But the two adventurers were already gone.

"Hmph," he snorted in displeasure, then tore off a piece of bread.

"By the way," he began.

"What's up?"

"Do you know what the fragrant olive means, in the language of flowers?"

The dinner consisted solely of High Elf Archer's favorite foods, but Goblin Slayer wasn't one to complain.

And when he had carried her up to the second floor of the tavern and paid for her room, requesting that the meal be put on her tab, he left the building.

§

He always knew what he had to do.

He constantly had to think, look ahead, stay vigilant, plan countermeasures and execute them.

What Goblin Slayer had to do at this moment was dig a hole.

It was night—the twin moons were already among the glinting stars filling the heavens.

All alone, he silently thrust the shovel into the ground, digging, digging.

The warmth from the wine helped ward off the chilly night breeze.

He was outside the town gate, on a footpath off the main road. It cut through a field, but not a wide, flat grassy plain. There were hills, copses of trees, reeds. Away from the road, the land was wild.

The place was largely deserted, which was why he'd chosen to dig his hole there.

It was about as deep as a person was tall. Not a dwarf or a rhea, but a human.

He lined the bottom with the thin sharpened stakes he had whittled and hid the opening with the earth he had dug out. The soil rested on a blanket over the mouth of the pit. At a glance, one would never suspect there was anything there.

He did this several times, then scattered small, bright stones around the area.

"Now then…"

The trouble was all the leftover soil.

Goblins could use it to strengthen the walls of their cave, and so wouldn't be bothered by it, but he didn't have the same luxury.

Doing landscaping by hand was quite troublesome for an adventurer.

Goblin Slayer put the earth into sacks he had prepared beforehand. Now they were sandbags.

He cinched up the mouths of the bags, then carried them two at a time, one on each shoulder.

He hid them in the rushes not far from the hole, building up a half circle.

It was uncertain whether this would help them later. But it couldn't hurt to be prepared for everything.

If nothing else, Goblin Slayer never begrudged necessary labor.

He piled the sandbags carefully, leaving no gaps, then finished by giving them a few smacks with the shovel to pack them in.

"…Mm."

Finally he nodded, satisfied.

It would do for the holes. The other places were all prepared. This had been the last.

All that was left was the trap he had built with the remaining stakes, the rope, and the wood, but there were only so many places he could set it up.

Goblin Slayer checked the sky, trying to judge how much time he had by the slant of the moons. The nights were long, and morning came late in fall and winter. Even so, he doubted he had much longer to work.

He quickly pulled the wooden boards out of his pack by their ties.

He moved over to shrubs and trees, doing some delicate work before he rose.

"Time to hurry."

He took up his baggage on his shoulders then ran under the moons like a shadow.

He was past the reeds and through the trees when it happened.

"Hey, what are you doing there?!"

A voice came slicing through the air like an ambush. Goblin Slayer stopped dead. .

There was the crunching of plants under boots, the scrape of them brushing against armor.

"Hm," Goblin Slayer muttered, but his hand did not move to his sword.

No goblin spoke the common tongue so fluently.

"Who's there?" he asked shortly. A rustle came as if in answer.

A tall person enveloped in an overcoat appeared.

The person's boots, just visible under the hem of the coat, were well used, the toes reinforced. Clearly an adventurer.

But the harsh voice that responded offered no answers.

"*I'm* asking the questions here."

The timbre caused Goblin Slayer to murmur, "A woman...?"

"...Once again. Who or what are you?"

Almost immediately, a white light, piercing to eyes adjusted to the dark, shot into the sky.

"I am Goblin Slayer."

With one finger he casually pushed away the blade at his throat.

He sounded put out, almost like he was fighting a yawn.

A long sword—blade one-sided—and a skilled sword fighter.

True, it had happened too quick for a response—but he had also *chosen* not to respond.

It would be foolish to ask who an opponent was and cut them down in the same breath.

Even one in the grip of bloodlust could understand that much.

Shrouded in her coat, the woman narrowed her eyes doubtfully.

"You…slay goblins…?"

"Yes."

"…Sounds insane."

"I see."

The blade he had pushed aside slid back, seeking his neck.

It lifted the chain with the silver tag that hung there.

"A silver rank tag… Silver-ranked adventurer?"

"It would seem," Goblin Slayer said with a nod, "the Guild has recognized me as such."

"…I see."

The sword retreated like a breath of wind and returned to its scabbard with a *click*.

The sheer smoothness of the motion suggested this was a high-ranking adventurer. Certainly at least Copper, Goblin Slayer guessed.

"It seems I was too hasty. My apologies."

"No, it's fine."

"I thought you were an undead or something…"

The woman sounded awkward as she apologized, but her tone had softened.

Goblin Slayer shook his head gently. It didn't particularly matter to him.

The problem was—

"Hey, don't I keep telling you not to do that?"

At that moment a voice, bright as the breaking of the sun, came from behind her.

"She jumps to the worst conclusions about everybody. Don't worry, I stopped her."

"The fact remains that he was suspicious."

The next voice was cold as cut ice. Two new people.

With a crinkle, the grass parted, producing a short adventurer also in an overcoat.

It would be easy to mistake this person for a rhea, but they carried a full-sized sword at their hip.

They must be human. A rhea wouldn't have the muscle to swing that weapon.

The other person carried a large staff and was dressed more smartly than the other two. Obviously a magic user of some type.

And all of them, to judge from their voices, were women. Parties composed entirely of women were relatively rare.

"So, what's the story? I'm curious myself," the diminutive swordswoman asked.

Before Goblin Slayer could say anything, she took a couple of nimble steps forward.

With a gait as lighthearted as her question, she closed the space between them as though she were out on a stroll.

"Hrm…," Goblin Slayer muttered, and after a moment's consideration, gave his answer.

"I am taking precautions."

"Precautions? Hmm…" She peered around Goblin Slayer, then said indifferently, "Strange equipment you've got…"

"Is it?"

"Ah, sorry. I don't mean to make fun of you. I just think it's amusing."

Her voice was so cheerful that Goblin Slayer could tell she was grinning under her hood.

Nonetheless, her clarification evoked no reaction from him. He had no idea what might be amusing about his grubby leather armor and cheap-looking helmet, or his sword and shield.

But as the women took stock of him, he scrutinized them in turn.

They were not from the local crowd of adventurers. And they were not goblins—of that, at least, he was sure.

"…I don't think he's involved. Most likely."

After a time, the adventurer with the staff spoke in her frigid tone.

"Frankly, I can hardly believe someone this weird even exists."

"I…suppose so. Granted he hides his face and skin, but I agree this seems a bit much."

The response came from the first woman. Her sword still in its scabbard, she continued in an oddly boastful tone, "I saw the difference in our abilities. He won't be a problem."

"You think? If you say so, I guess it must be true."

The girl, who had cocked her head while her companions discussed, ended by clapping her hands.

"Well, mister, sorry to bother you!"

"It's fine." Goblin Slayer shook his head slightly, then set his cargo on the ground. "Did you come to see the festival?"

"Huh? Oh, uh, well… I guess so. It's just near here, right?"

"Yes." Goblin Slayer nodded. "This is the town that will hold the harvest festival." Then, after a moment's thought, he added, "If you need an inn, you had best get one soon."

"Oh, wow. Okay. I see. It's pretty late now. We'd better get going. Sorry!" she added one last time, and pattered lightly away.

The other two hurriedly collected themselves as she slipped farther and farther away.

"Argh, she's always—! We shall take our leave of you, then. Apologies for the trouble."

"Sorry."

The other two followed the departing girl, melting away like shadows. Goblin Slayer, now alone, simply muttered, "Hm."

He had placed a small stone where the short swordswoman had stood just a moment ago.

As he recalled, it was the exact spot where he had dug and concealed a hole.

Was it martial training, the way she walked, magic, or simply luck? He didn't know.

And speaking of things he didn't know, he couldn't determine why the women had been using this footpath and not the main road.

"……"

But thinking about it brought him no answers, so he simply dismissed the question.

They were almost certainly just adventurers who had come from elsewhere to see the festival.

And they were not goblins. That was enough.

Still, he had felt sure that people would not come through this area…

"…I'll have to pick my places even more carefully."

There was much to do.

And he always knew what must be done.

The feather pen scraped along the sheepskin paper under the candlelight.

An honor though it was, she couldn't help feeling she lacked the wherewithal for this great responsibility.

If asked how much she had learned outside the Temple, she would have no ready answer.

It was an immense thing to write the prayer to be offered to the goddess.

"*Sigh...* Everyone before me did such a great job..."

She eyed the clothes she had just received, piled in a corner of the room, and exhaled.

She saw them each year, and while they always captured her heart, she had never imagined that she herself might be wearing them so soon.

What can I say about the goddess?

Should it be different from the prayers they offered daily? What even was a prayer?

"What would *he* say...?"

The vision of an expressionless steel helmet flashed through her mind, and she couldn't repress a gentle smile.

I'll say what I've seen. That's all I have.

".........All right."

I'll do my best. With that decision, letters began flowing onto the page.

Her penmanship was not excellent, but the words were no one's but hers.

CHAPTER 3

THE HARVEST FESTIVAL BRINGS DREAMS

Pew! Pew! The morning sky filled with lazy bursts of colored smoke.

It must have been hired wizards putting on a fireworks show. The scintillating colors made their skill apparent.

Things would be busy despite the early hour, so the perkiest performance groups were already up and playing music. The ruckus carried even to the farm, a good distance from town, brushing past Cow Girl's ears.

The weather was beautiful, and it was festival day—the harvest festival, the autumn festival.

Her heart was light, dancing in her chest. She was in high spirits, altogether too happy to sit still.

"Oooh... Ummm... Ohhh..."

Or at least, that's how she should have felt.

But there was a reason she was in her room in her underwear, groaning.

Her little closet hung open, clothes littering the room from door to bed. There was hardly a place to walk.

And in the middle of it all crouched Cow Girl.

Her hair was a mess. After all the effort she had put into straightening it, now she would have to run a brush through it again later.

But that was a minor problem.

She had never been much for makeup. She might straighten her hair, put on a little powder and a touch of rouge, but that would be it.

So the problem was—

"I have no idea what to wear!"

This was critical.

Would a dress be good? Or should she try to play it more casual? Or should she go bold?

"Can't wear my work clothes… Or can I? Just plain and simple?"

Ah, but one thing, exactly one thing was certain.

"*He*'ll be dressed the way he always is!"

Grimy leather armor and shabby helmet, carrying a sword not long but not short, with a round shield fastened to his arm.

He would be wearing his normal clothes (?), and she hers, and that was how they would go to the festival together. They would go to the festival together!

While she had been holding her head with one hand, the work clothes had found their way into the other. She tossed them into the hamper. *Bye.*

Leftover were outfits she had assembled bit by bit on her occasional days off.

But none of them seemed reasonable. There was nothing she could wear now, when it counted.

Tragically, she just didn't have enough experience points in everyday matters. Her level was too low.

It was clearly too late for regrets, but she wished she had tried to be more fashionable on a regular basis.

"Maybe… Maybe I don't need to worry about underwear…"

Yeah. That would be all right. For sure.

—No! You need to figure out your regular clothes, never mind your underwear! Argh, I'm getting confused!

She thought she had heard once that when you were this confused, the important thing was to not show it.

Letting out an involuntary little scream, she picked up one article of clothing after another, deemed each not quite appropriate, and tossed it aside.

Then she wondered if the thing she had most recently discarded might actually be best, grabbed it again, and put it to her chest, only to throw it away once more.

Her date with him was in the morning. All this fretting was wasting valuable time.

She was so preoccupied with these concerns that she didn't hear her uncle's knock.

"...Ahem. Excuse me. Is now a good time?"

"Oh! Eep! Uh...oh... Dadd—I mean, Uncle?!"

She dove for her bed and wound the blanket around to cover herself. When she checked, the door was still shut. She put a hand to her ample chest to calm her pounding heart.

"O-okay. Come in."

"Pardon me. What...? What is all this?"

Her uncle could hardly be blamed for his sigh as he entered the room.

She didn't even try to make an excuse, but only averted her eyes from the mess in embarrassment.

"Planning to open your own clothing store...?"

"Ha... Ha-ha-ha."

She scratched her cheek in a gesture of unmistakable embarrassment toward her exasperated uncle.

"...Just make sure you clean it up," he said. He didn't have to add anything else. "Anyway, I...hm. Now's a good time. I have something for you."

"Huh? What's that?"

In response to her puzzlement, he offered her a startling blue dress. The dazzling colored cloth was decorated with lace and embroidery.

Her uncle's expression was difficult to describe, except for the wistful reflection in his eyes.

"My little sister...your mother wore this when she was your age."

"Oh...!"

She thought it was truly beautiful. She took it and held it tentatively in front of herself, to see how it looked.

"I wonder if I can wear it. Will it look good on me...?"

"It'll be perfect," her uncle said. "Your mother had longer hair, but otherwise you're her spitting image."

"R-right. Right! I'll try it on."

Mommy wore this? Do I...look like her?

Inexpressible feelings welled up at that thought, and she hugged the dress to herself tightly.

"Careful, it'll wrinkle."

"Oh, r-right… Gotta watch out. But… Hee-hee-hee!"

She had all but smashed it against her huge chest, and now she hurriedly smoothed it out again so it would stay neat.

The smile on her face, however, she couldn't help. She spoke her next words sincerely.

"Thank you, Uncle!"

He blinked and raised his eyes to the ceiling for several seconds before shaking his head.

"…It's nothing. Don't mention it." And then his craggy face softened just a bit. "It belonged to your mother, after all. Now it's yours. Wear it with love."

"I will! I'll treasure it."

As he closed the door, her uncle warned her not to hurry and trip in it, to which she responded at the top of her lungs, "I won't!"

Then she flung off the blanket around her and tried on her mother's dress.

The billowing skirt felt a bit alien to a girl used to wearing farm clothes.

But the foreign sensation also brought home the fact that she was breaking the routine, and that was exciting.

She donned a hat with a big ribbon to accompany the dress.

This'll do it!

She spun around in a quick inspection of her appearance. There was no mirror to look in—but then, a girl couldn't have everything.

The only issue was her shoes, which weren't very stylish…

But this is enough to make me a proper lady, anyway!

"All right, let's go!"

She threw open the door. But she saw only her uncle waiting in the kitchen.

He had the milk out and seemed to be in the middle of something.

"Uncle, it's festival day. You're not going to go out…?"

"I'm too old for that sort of thing. I'll stay here with the whaddaya call it—ice crème." He had learned how to make the frozen treat, but frowned as his mouth formed the unfamiliar name. "What about you? Not going to stay out the whole day?"

"Nah. What if you need to go out? We can't just leave the farm alone."

"That so?" he murmured as she waved good-bye.

She was a bit distracted that he seemed to want to say something, but...

"See you later!"

"Mm. See you. Be careful."

She was out of time. Cow Girl went quickly out the door.

The sky was blue, the smoke from the fireworks clearing. The autumn sun washed over their hill, and the wind swept by in a rush.

And there he was, standing in the sun, scanning the area as he always did.

Just as she'd expected, he wore all his usual equipment. The dirty armor, the low-quality helmet, the sword of a strange length, and the round shield.

Ah, but—

I'm different today!

"Hey! Sorry to keep you waiting."

"Not at all."

She waved to him, trying to act as casual as possible.

He returned with his usual bland answer, then cocked his head in thought before adding, "I haven't been waiting very long."

"Oh yeah?"

"Yes."

"Let's go, then!"

"Yes."

He nodded, then prepared to set off ahead of her at his routine brisk pace.

But before he could, Cow Girl spun and seized his leather-gloved hand.

"Erk..."

"It's gonna be crowded. You wouldn't want to get separated, would you?"

Even to Cow Girl herself, it smacked of pretext. She wished her voice wouldn't scratch.

Maybe his gloves would stop him from noticing her pulse pounding through her palm...

It was hard to say if he was aware of her feelings. Perplexed, he said, "It may be crowded...in town."

"W-well, it can't hurt to be prepared." Cow Girl glanced away and scratched her cheek with her free hand. She could feel the heat on her fingertips. She must have been bright red. "I mean, we need to kind of—get used to it." She grabbed the brim of her hat and adjusted it so he wouldn't see her blush. She gently adjusted her grip on his hand. "Because I'm—I'm not used to it."

"I see." He nodded. "That is important."

Cow Girl nodded, too, and walked along with her hand in his.

"...H-hey."

"What is it?"

"Uh, I mean—" Gazing straight ahead, Cow Girl asked what she had been dying to ask. "My clothes—I mean...what do you think?"

"..."

It was the same road they always walked on. The same scenery they always saw.

The same him. A different her. Holding hands.

The same silence he always lapsed into when he thought. Then—

"They suit you. I think, anyway."

It was enough to make her every step lighter than air.

"...Hee-hee-hee!"

Cow Girl felt like she might just float up to the sky.

§

It was a flood of sound.

Horns blew, drums pounded, flutes sang, and footsteps and laughter filled the streets.

Shopkeepers called out, street performers yelled, and the voices of passersby rolled past in waves.

It was palpable in the air even before they reached the town gate, but inside, things were on an entirely different level.

"I know they do this every year," she said, grasping his glove tightly, still blushing, "but it's always amazing."

"Yes."

His helmet moved in response.

Today of all days, his strange equipment didn't stand out too much. After all, everywhere they looked, performers danced in the street and put on impromptu shows. And there were more than a few visiting adventurers who didn't remove their equipment in town.

If anything, it was Cow Girl who drew all the attention.

An elegant young woman was holding hands with an adventurer in a grimy helmet and armor. Curious eyes followed her one after another.

I wonder how I look to them.

She enjoyed the passing thought.

Maybe they thought she was an aristocrat mingling with the populace, and he was her bodyguard.

No... I guess that's a little much.

She was the niece—the adopted daughter—of a local farm owner who had a fair amount of land to his name.

And her companion was a known veteran around these parts, a Silver-ranked adventurer.

Of course they all knew that she was no young noble. And yet...

"Guess I had a pretty good idea."

"Of what?"

She snickered at his questioning helmet, then made a show of straightening her hat.

"Where you would take me first."

"Hm."

He stared up at the sky silently, thinking. The stream of people broke around them as they stood still like rocks in a river.

They weren't really in anyone's way. She waited for his response, smiling.

After a moment, he murmured as if in sudden realization:

"I haven't had breakfast yet."

"Oh," she said, putting her hand over her open mouth.

He was right.

She had been so concerned with her clothes and preparations that the morning meal had slipped her mind.

He gazed at her unflinchingly as she covered her eyes.

"Shall we get something at a stall?"

"...Yeah. That sounds good," she agreed.

She felt bad for her uncle, but it was too late for that now.

He was right there with her. She would start by apologizing to him.

"...I'm sorry. I just kinda...totally forgot."

"No." He shook his head slowly. And then, after a moment, he added, "These things happen."

She enjoyed peering into the stalls and wondering where they would eat, but eventually, she couldn't stand her hunger any longer.

The late breakfast they finally got from one of the vendors was surprisingly expensive for what it was. Fried thick-cut bacon mixed with potatoes. That was all.

But it was simply delicious.

"Oh!" she said, laughing. "This is our bacon!"

"Is it?" he replied, inserting some food through the visor of his helmet. "I see."

The salty, greasy potatoes delighted her tongue.

She wolfed down her breakfast, blowing on the food to keep from burning her mouth.

He ate steadily, silently, but neatly—as he always did.

Then they took the empty, unglazed plates and shattered them before setting off again.

Lively voices called to them from every side.

"Plum brandy for the lovely couple? Melts in your mouth!" cried a liquor vendor. Cow Girl stopped there.

"What do you think?" he asked, pointing. "Do you want a drink?" Well, since they were here...

They were presented with two cups of a faintly sweet-smelling fruit liqueur in small earthenware vessels.

She sipped hers daintily. He, however, swallowed his in a single gulp.

"Won't it go to your head if you drink it all at once like that?"

"It's not a problem," he said very seriously. "Brandy wakes you up."

"…Isn't that just a way of saying you're kind of out of it right now?"

"It's not a way of saying anything."

"Oh, really?" She detected a slightly cornered tone in his voice and snickered.

She was just teasing, just joking. If he had really been feeling ill, she would certainly have noticed. And then she would have dragged him back to his bed and tucked him in.

The festival was fun, yes—but all the more reason she didn't want to ruin it by pushing him too hard.

"You sure were out late last night, though. What were you doing?"

"Finishing up something that needed to be done."

She was all too used to these non-explanations by now. But she didn't press him further, simply saying, "Huh."

Warmth was spreading through her chest, and she was starting to feel cheery. She wasn't sure if it was the alcohol.

"I thought you were asleep," he said in the same aloof tone as ever. Did he notice how she was feeling? "Were you awake that whole time?"

"Oh, haha… I just kinda…couldn't sleep."

"I see."

He didn't press her, either. Together they merged back into the swirling, celebrating crowd.

There was never enough time.

An elf archer tossed plates into the air and shot them down to boisterous applause. A dwarf had set up a stall selling beautiful engraved swords he said he had made himself. A rhea musician played a stirring tune for all to hear.

Wherever they went, the familiar town had something new to show them.

They had been walking around for a while when he suddenly stopped.

"Huh? What's up?"

She peered into his face but, of course, could see no expression there. He only muttered, "Hm." Then—

"…Wait a moment."

"Well, sure, but…"

He pulled his gloved hand away from hers.

Suddenly alone, she did what she always did and leaned against a wall while she waited for him.

She held up her now empty hand in front of her face and breathed gently on it. She wasn't exactly lonely or upset. But as she watched the throng of adventurers and travelers flow by, a thought occurred to her.

This relationship of him going, her waiting was not likely to change.

This was how it would always be.

They had seen different things.

Ten years.

Ten years since she had left her home and their village had been destroyed.

Five years since she had been reunited with him, now an adventurer.

She didn't know how he had spent the five years they had been apart. She knew nothing of the days before he became Goblin Slayer. She didn't even know what had happened in their village. She had heard the stories, of course, but that was only secondhand.

She remembered holding her uncle's hand as empty caskets were put in the ground.

But that was all.

She didn't really know what had happened, or why, or where everyone had gone.

Had there been fire? The fields, what about them? The animals? Her friends? Her father. Her mother.

What about the bird's nest she had kept her own little secret, the treasure she had hidden in the knot of a tree?

Her mother's apron, the one Cow Girl had been promised once she got older? Her favorite shoes? The cup she had gotten for her birthday, whose green color had faded though she had taken such care of it.

One after another, the precious memories came back to her, now almost like ghosts.

What did she have left? One small box, with the things she had found in town that day and determined to bring with her.

If—it was just her imagining. But if.

If she hadn't left the village that day, what would have happened to her? Would she have seen the same things he did and survived?

Or would she have died and left him alone? And if so, would he have taken vengeance for her?

Or… What if *he* had died, and she had been the one to live?

What a terrible thought.

At that moment she heard, "Sorry to keep you waiting." The familiar armored form appeared before her out of the crowd.

"No problem."

She shook her head as she straightened her hat. He held a small object out to her.

"What's this?" she said, peering at it.

"When we were small…in the village," he murmured, "you liked things like this."

He was holding out a small, handcrafted ring.

It was silver—or it appeared to be, anyway. She knew it had to be imitation silver. Something a roadside vendor had cooked up to part children from their pocket change.

In other words, just a toy.

She found herself smiling. Then laughing.

"Ha-ha-ha! …That was when I was a girl."

"Was it?" he said in a small, clipped voice. And then, "I guess it was."

"Yeah."

She nodded. Nodded, and put on the ring.

It may have been handcrafted, but it was cheaply made. It didn't even have a fake gem. Just a metal band.

But it caught the sunlight and glittered, bright enough to make her squint.

"…But," she whispered, "I still like them."

"…Do you?"

"Yeah."

"Thank you," she managed to squeeze out, and then Cow Girl slipped the ring into the pocket of her dress.

She kept her left hand on it so that she wouldn't lose it—her right hand, of course, was in his.

"Shall we?"

She smiled and started off, hand in hand.

She couldn't see his face behind his helmet. But…

…He was smiling, too. She was pretty sure.

She trusted he was.

§

It was almost noon when a voice called out to the two of them.

"Well, if it isn't old man Gob Killer!"

Cow Girl craned her neck to see who it was even as she fretted about what to do with her ring.

She didn't recognize the relatively high-pitched voice, but the recipient seemed to.

The helmet turned around to look squarely at Scout Boy, who was pointing at them.

Beside him were the rhea Druid Girl, Rookie Warrior, and Apprentice Priestess.

Cow Girl realized the young adventurers even spent their time off together.

"Whoa, dude, are you on a date with the farm girl?!"

"Hey, you should be more polite to someone so much older!"

Rookie Warrior sounded very interested indeed, but Apprentice Priestess tugged on his sleeve.

Gob Killer? Leave it to a kid to come up with a nickname like that. Cow Girl smiled.

She grinned up at his helmet in a deliberately meaningful gesture.

"A date? I wonder. What do you think?"

"Hold on," he said bluntly. "I'm only twenty."

Her smile widened. He hadn't denied it.

"Whaaaa?!"

The boys gave strange shrieks, and finally Cow Girl couldn't hold herself back any longer.

"He sure is. But no one knows since he always has that helmet of his on."

"…It's a necessary measure."

His voice sounded a bit more brusque than usual.

He was *pouting.* Her day kept getting better and better.

Everyone said they didn't know what he was thinking because they couldn't see his face. But for someone who had known him as long as she had, it was easy enough.

"Um, could you…give us some help?" Apprentice Priestess asked them hesitantly.

Vwip. Goblin Slayer's steel helmet turned toward her.

"Is it goblins?"

"No, not at all. Umm…"

"Oh…not goblins?"

His dull reply left Druid Girl glancing around uncertainly.

Next to her, Scout Boy said, "You're pretty dense, man!" and guffawed. "No way any goblins are showing up here!"

"They will."

"Huh?!"

"Goblins will come."

"Really?!"

Yes. What? No way! Back and forth they went. Cow Girl watched them with a sort of helpless amusement.

"Let boys be boys. Did you two need something?"

She crouched down to eye level for Druid Girl and Apprentice Priestess.

They glanced at each other, then at Cow Girl's chest, emphasized by the arm she was resting under it.

Then they each looked down at themselves and sighed. Easy enough to understand.

"Don't worry. You'll keep growing."

"…That's not really reassuring."

"Yeah, it's still…"

The two of them got red-faced and fidgety, staring hard at the ground.

Cow Girl smiled inside as she gave them both a pat on the head.

"Anyway, what's on your minds?"

The girls nodded, then glanced back and pointed at the entrance to a tavern behind them.

A huge crowd had gathered there, and in the middle of the circle was a small table. On top of the table was a statue of an open-mouthed frog.

A drunk was standing at a white line drawn on the road, holding a jangling handful of silver balls.

"Hrah! Yaah! Haaah!"

He flung the balls one after another, but to no avail. Each one bounced off the table and onto the ground.

The shop owner standing next to the statue gathered up the balls with practiced ease and said in a loud voice:

"Step right up, ten balls for one bronze coin! Land one, get a mug of ale! Or lemonade for the boys and girls!"

"They won't go in," Scout Boy said with a huff.

He had been training with Heavy Warrior's party, but he was still a child. Fifteen was the minimum age to become an adventurer, and that would have been several years before for this boy, but he still could not have been twenty yet.

Cow Girl realized he must have lied about his age, but she felt no inclination to bring that up.

"Yeah. I think those silver balls are rigged."

"Now, now, kid. That's not funny."

The trainee warrior spoke half in jest as he handed over a bronze coin, and the owner responded with a smile and a tone that suggested he'd had this conversation before.

Then the two boys tossed the balls one after another, but they came nowhere near the target.

A great *sigh*… came from the girls with them.

"…They get caught up in these things so easily."

"Boys stink, huh?"

They weren't much more mature, but they tried to pretend they were.

Cow Girl heard out the girls' complaints with an "Uh-huh, uh-huh."

Boys. They're trying to look cool…

"…and girls want them to," she said, glancing at her old friend.

The expression behind the steel helmet was, as ever, impossible to see and yet easy to guess.

"What is it?"

"Give us a demonstration?"

"Hrm."

Goblin Slayer swept his gaze over the four children and Cow Girl.

Then, with a small nod, he pulled a bronze coin from his pouch and went up to the tavern owner.

"Shopkeep."

"Yessir!"

"One, please."

What happened next was almost too quick for the eye to follow.

He rolled the balls around in his palm with a *clink*, then tossed them into the frog's mouth.

There was nothing unusual about his technique.

He simply had his mark. But he was precise, and fast.

One went in. Two. Three, four. Then five and six.

For several seconds, the balls rolling down into the frog statue created a sound much like a *ribbit*.

"Wow!"

"Whoa…"

The amazement on the children's faces was plain to see.

And not just the children.

The onlookers *ooh*ed appreciatively and began to clap.

Heh! Cow Girl stuck out her ample chest almost as if she were the one who had put on this stunning display.

People thought he was only good for goblin slaying.

But that wasn't true. There was more to him than that.

"Geez, mister, ya couldn't have held back? For my sake?"

"No."

As he made his deeply serious reply to the owner, Cow Girl gave him a congratulatory pat on the back.

"You always were good at these games, even when we were kids."

"Yes."

There had been a tavern in their hometown as well, although the statue had not been a frog, but a woman with a water jug. At each festival, he had won three glasses of lemonade for her, himself, and his sister.

Come to think of it, I remember him practicing skipping stones in the river before every festival.

She realized with a rush of fondness that he had always been the type to prepare thoroughly.

"Wow, way to go, man!" a server said. "Six lemonades? Coming right up!"

"Yes."

He dipped his helmet once, just as he always did.

Then he turned to the boys and explained in a measured tone.

"And that is what you do."

"...R-right."

"Now you try."

Goblin Slayer passed the four remaining silver balls to the young boys with a jangle.

Scout Boy took two, at once frantic and stoic.

"D-don't you have any other advice?"

"Practice."

That was all he said.

"Bleh," the boys whined. Goblin Slayer nodded at them and stood seriously.

"G-give it your best shot!"

"Hey, you gotta throw better than that!"

"Ha-ha-ha! Aww, don't be so hard on him."

So the girls watched the three boys—

"Oh..."

Cow Girl realized it wasn't wrong to think of him with that word.

Was it strange?

No, it wasn't. It really wasn't.

Of course, it had been ten years since then. It was a lot of time to build experience. She had learned just as many things as he had.

But all that was just an accumulation.

The roots are still the same.

That was a principle she believed in... No—it was something she hoped was true.

"Drink?"

"Sure, thanks."

She took the cold glass from his hand. It was well water with lemon and honey in it.

That refreshing chill, she thought, hadn't changed in ten years.

"Oh, yeah," she said, pretending something had just occurred to her as she watched the children determinedly toss the little balls out of the corner of her eye. "Since you got it for me, why don't you put it on me? The ring."

"Where?"

He gazed intently at her fingers from her thumb to her pinky.

"I mean…my ring finger," she said, starting to regret she had said anything. "…How about it?"

"On which hand?"

"What do you mean, which? The—"

The left hand.

She shook her head, somehow unable to get the words out.

"Ri—"

She took a breath and searched in her pocket, pulling the ring out with her left hand.

"Right hand…please."

"All right."

And then he put the ring on her finger without a hint of ceremony.

She held it up to the sun, and it gleamed brightly.

Well, I guess I'll have to take it off when I work.

But at least for the festival, she could leave it on.

With the sweet-sour taste of the lemonade in her mouth, Cow Girl resolved to have all the fun she could.

©Noboru Kannatuki

§

Now, let us leave behind the frog statue outside the door and follow the shopkeeper inside as he goes into the tavern for more lemonade.

"I shall not stick my nose in too far, but…" Lizard Priest nibbled luxuriously on a fried sausage covered with copious amounts of cheese. It was not rude in lizard culture to talk while enjoying one's food. "I wonder if it will go well… Of course, I certainly hope it will."

"Ahh, things in this world turn out for the best eight or nine times out of ten," said Dwarf Shaman, pounding his belly like a drum as he took a gulp of his stiff drink and proclaimed, "It's fine!" He glanced to the side with a sly smile as he said, "What I'm really worried about is…"

The last person at the table, High Elf Archer, glared like she was hunting prey.

"Grrr…"

"What are you groaning about, Long-Ears?"

"Because!" She pounded the table, pointing outside the tavern as her ears flounced. "I tried that earlier, and I didn't get a single one in!"

"All that means is that shooting and throwing are different things."

"It's not fair! I'm a high elf! We're descendants of the gods!"

Then she took a desperate swig of her lemonade.

She had blown one bronze coin after another and still ended up having to purchase her own drink. It was the sourest lemonade she'd ever had.

"Well, such is the way of the world. Milady Ranger and milord Goblin Slayer have different talents."

Lizard Priest's tone suggested he was talking to a child. And Dwarf Shaman was only too happy to add his opinion.

"Sure it ain't just that you're sore about losing to Beard-cutter?"

"*Sniiiiff*… I-I'm not sore."

Lizard Priest hissed with amusement as High Elf Archer ground out the words between her teeth.

"…Oh, wait a second."

The elf suddenly flitted her ears in surprise, raising her head and turning to the window.

"Something the matter, milady Ranger?"

"Look out. They're moving."

She was right. The two of them were leaving the ball game behind.

Cow Girl shuffled regretfully, while Goblin Slayer strode as boldly as ever.

"Um, they're saying… 'Say hi to Guild Girl for me' and 'Yes.'"

Can't he think of anything friendlier to say?

High Elf Archer puffed out her cheeks in annoyance, playing with her lemonade glass, now covered in condensation.

Dwarf Shaman stroked his beard, seemingly amused by this.

"I can't think of a sillier use for an elf's ears."

"Oh? Don't you know anything about human culture, dwarf?" High Elf Archer gave him an unusual and confident smile, her ears standing straight up. "If you can do silly things, it shows you have enough resources to afford the luxury."

"Sounds to me like the excuse of someone who got so caught up in what she was doing that she forgot her purse someplace."

"That has nothing to do with this."

"This is why I hate elves! Always trying to hide their problems."

"Strong words when dwarves can only ever think about money!"

And then the two friends were off again on one of their usual arguments.

Lizard Priest watched them in pleasure, slapping his tail on the floor. He waved down a nearby waitress.

"Excuse me, Miss Server!"

"Yes, sir!"

The attentive response came from a padfoot—a beast girl. Her hands, feet, and ears were those of an animal. She bustled over to him.

"My." Naturally, Lizard Priest's eyes widened a bit as he recognized the girl who stood there, chuckling.

"Pardon me, but are you not one of the Guild's girls?"

"Oh, yes. I'm working two jobs." Padfoot Girl hid her smile with a tray, but couldn't conceal her laugh. "Look around. Everyone's so busy today, they'll take all the help they can get."

"I see, I see. I'm glad this rising tide seems to be lifting your boat as well." Lizard Priest nodded somberly, using one of his sharp claws to indicate the menu on the wall. "I request another two or three of your fried sausages. And if you could ensure the cheese is especially copious…"

"Sure, sure. By the way, if you want, we have sausages with herbs in them, too."

"Ah, herbs, you say?"

"And others with cartilage…"

"Indeed!"

"Plus some stuffed with cheese!"

"Oh, my!"

Needless to say, his eyes had never sparkled brighter.

So lunchtime passed uneventfully.

Goodness, goodness, goodness. My, my. Another dear visitor to our shrine.

Yes, at the ritual for the harvest festival we will—yes, we ask for the gods' power.

Call God is not the highest of miracles.

It seeks to borrow just a fragment of the gods' power to ensure peace and a good harvest.

Yes, so it's the perfect opportunity for one who wishes to walk on the astral plane.

You—go and call that girl. Yes, right. I believe she's in town at the moment.

In any case, I think she is quite promising.

She is modest and pious, and able to use three miracles even though she is still just Obsidian rank.

Thus why I requested her to lead the ritual at the festival this year.

She is a good girl. But there's…just a small problem…

What? You ask of connections to the dark elves or the Demon Lord? Reincarnated shrine maidens? Secrets to her birth?

Heavens, I think you have read altogether too much into our chat.

She is hardly that sort of Platinum-ranked material… And anyway, isn't her story quite common enough? If you'll excuse my saying so.

Regardless, I think of her like a daughter. Oh, but don't tell anyone I said that.

It's just… How do I put this…?

There is a bit of an issue with the adventurer who accompanies her…

Does he seem suspicious? Ha-ha-ha, oh, no.

That person would never worship the Dark Gods—of that alone I am certain.

If he had the time for such things, he would put it to better use.

What? You saw a strange adventurer on your way here?

One that made you think an undead had possessed a suit of living armor?

………

Oh… Goddess…

No, not at all. He is not a bad person.

…Now then, I believe you have heard the story from the archbishop in the water town…

We will certainly do anything in our power to help, O brave Hero.

CHAPTER 4

It's Your Smile That Matters

Noontime on a festival day saw the plaza packed with people, giving the appearance of a living mosaic.

The pillar that stood in the middle of the plaza in lieu of a clock tower made a natural meeting point.

She looked somewhat plain amid the gaudily dressed men and women milling about.

She was wearing a neat but unremarkable white blouse. She had put on culottes that were made for ease of movement above all else, and plain tights. Her hair was styled the same way as usual. But she had gotten a new ribbon to hold her braid back.

Simple, personal clothes—this was all she had to wear into town on her day off.

After all…

"Ah."

…See?

It was then he came, striding boldly through the crowd as though it were not there.

There was no mistaking him, and certainly no losing him in the sea of bodies. He had his tarnished leather armor and steel helmet. His sword and shield.

He was so utterly his usual self it was enough to make her laugh.

So she summoned up a smile just like the one she always had. Only her clothing was different today.

"Did you enjoy your morning?"

"Yes," Goblin Slayer said dispassionately, coming to a stop in front of her and giving one of his usual nods. "Sorry to keep you waiting."

"It's all right. I just got here myself."

A small lie on her part.

She wouldn't mention that she had been so excited she had arrived before noon.

She coughed a little to cover her deception and continued.

"...Hee-hee. You are a little late, though, Mr. Goblin Slayer."

"Sorry."

"Not at all, it's fine. After all, I..."

...*like waiting.*

Then Guild Girl smiled mischievously, spun, and began to lead him away.

Her braid, bright with its new ribbon, wagged like a tail.

"Well, let's go, then!"

She knew. Even if she had dressed up, it wouldn't have gotten his attention.

Instead, she wanted him to see the real her, not the face she showed at work every day.

Not Guild Girl. Just regular Girl. The way she normally was.

Part of the reason she had dressed plainly was to declare, *This is me!*

"Did you eat lunch already?"

"No." Goblin Slayer shook his head slowly. "Not yet."

"Okay, then..."

Vwip, vwip. She turned her head so quickly you could practically hear it.

She considered one plan after another, compared them, dismissed some, and finally chose one.

She knew stew was one of his favorite foods—the way they'd made it in his village, of course.

She couldn't compete in that area. But she could take advantage of the festival day.

"How about we walk while we eat?" she said, smiling shyly. "I know it's not good manners, but today is special…"

"I don't mind."

"I knew you wouldn't. Okay then, let's get something and then have a look around…"

She glanced up, taking in his face from below. The stained helmet. The same face she saw every day.

"But where, I wonder?"

"Hrm."

"We can go to a place you like, you know?"

"Mm."

Goblin Slayer grunted once. Guild Girl smiled at him.

Waiting didn't bother her. Not so long as the other person was trying to respond to her, anyway.

From the five years of their acquaintance, she understood that he was thinking carefully.

Then, after a moment, Goblin Slayer nodded and answered.

"Let's start here, then."

"Sure!"

He set off at his bold pace, and she followed him like an excited puppy.

She might have been able to get away with holding his hand so they wouldn't get separated.

But she knew she would never lose sight of this singular, unforgettable person.

Guild Girl was determined to enjoy escorting him for the afternoon. She trailed after him, her smile growing ever wider.

§

The two of them bought candied apples from a stall selling sweets.

It didn't exactly pass for a full meal, but one could hardly complain about festival food.

That was what she thought, anyway, and she couldn't imagine him being dissatisfied with any food.

Speaking of things I can't imagine…

He ate the treat easily without removing his helmet, a feat she might not otherwise have considered possible.

"…Hee-hee."

"What?" His helm tilted in a quizzical expression as he broke the now bare stick in two.

"Nothing," Guild Girl said, shaking her head and not trying to hide her smile. "I was just wondering if there was any food you won't eat."

At her question, Goblin Slayer *hmm*ed and lapsed into thought.

Guild Girl watched him out of the corner of her eye as she licked her apple. *Mm. Sweet.*

"I suppose I would eat it if I had to," he muttered, and she followed with a soft "Yes?"

"But I prefer to avoid fish."

"Fish?"

"They are easy enough to get if there is a river nearby, but rivers also mean parasites, and the possibility of food poisoning." There was a pause, and then he added, "And they stink."

"That's true," she agreed with a laugh. Even smoked, dried, or salted fish had a very distinctive odor. "I understand. I've seen adventurers arguing about that very thing."

"Oh?"

"Somebody bought preserved fish for provisions, and they got into a big fight over whether it smelled too terrible."

She was exaggerating a little, but he nodded and said, "I see."

Now, which party could it have been?

She remembered the incident, but couldn't quite recall their faces.

Adventurers were generally rather unmoored and scoundrel-esque.

Some might seem to make a home, yet if they suddenly pulled up roots one day, no one would give it a second thought. He, or she, or they, would simply go to some pleasant new town and do fine for themselves.

It was only natural, after all.

A fresh start offered much greater relief than facing the fact that everyone else in the party died because of their own failure to do their job. Regularly encountering all those other adventurers day in and day out, how could they help thinking about it?

It doesn't bear much thought…

That person you hadn't seen recently—was he dead?

The one you just talked to before she left on an adventure—would you ever see her again?

Waiting was only easy when you were absolutely sure the other person would come back.

But if you weren't…

"However, it is effective in smoking out a nest."

He was making some serious point—he was always serious—oblivious to her thoughts.

Guild Girl knew he wasn't joking, yet she smiled.

Ever since they had set out for the afternoon, he—or rather, they—had been like this.

Each time there was a choice of directions he would scan from right to left. When they passed a sewer grate, he would stomp down on it with a *clang*.

They came to the end of the main street and walked along the riverbank, where she stared up- and downstream.

The burbling of the river, the splash of jumping fish, the boats that skirted along the water—none of it seemed to catch his attention.

"Mmm, isn't this lovely?"

Guild Girl closed her eyes as the cool autumn breeze kissed her cheeks.

Then she grabbed onto the guardrail of the bridge and leaned out as far as she could over the water.

"You'll fall." To her, the brusque comment was simply evidence that he was paying attention to her.

"I'm fine," she said, spinning back around.

Hands supporting her against the guardrail, she arched her back and leaned out into space.

Her braided hair danced as the wind caught it.

"This river must run all the way to the sea."

"That's right," he said. "It starts in the mountains."

"But it's nothing like the water town. What did you think of that place?"

"The streets were confusing," Goblin Slayer said without emotion. "Good for defense, but troublesome when trying to go somewhere."

"You mean we better be careful goblins don't get into this town, either."

"Yes." Goblin Slayer nodded. "Exactly."

Then…

"Oh."

Just for a second, Guild Girl met the eyes of a sightseer on a boat passing under the bridge.

A lovely girl with beautiful golden hair and pale cheeks tinted a light red.

She was not wearing her usual gold armor. Today she was sporting a navy blue dress.

Next to her was a large man with a severe and somewhat confused expression on his face. The woman must have been Female Knight.

"…Hee-hee."

The knight put a finger to her lips and glared at Guild Girl as if to demand this remain their secret. Guild Girl couldn't help laughing at seeing the adventurer behave like any other girl at her young age.

Yes. Yes, of course. Our secret.

She figured everyone else was already well aware of the situation, but her lips were sealed.

It seemed to be going well for the two of them. That was the important thing. *Now then, I wonder what everyone thinks of us.*

"Say, Mr. Goblin Slayer." She came away from the railing and tugged on his arm. "Where should we go next?"

"Hrm…"

With a curt throaty sound, he set off at his usual gait, Guild Girl behind him with her chest out proudly.

Here, there—he changed directions seemingly on a whim, but he walked with such confidence that she assumed he had something in mind.

She was enjoying the simple mystery of where they were going, what they would do there.

He stopped several bends in the road later, where they emerged onto a busy thoroughfare.

"Oh, this is where all the performers are, isn't it?"

Artists of every stripe in every costume imaginable proclaimed their artistry for all to hear.

Passersby smiled, enjoyed the shows, clapped, and left a tip—or ignored the whole spectacle and moved along.

A rhea musician coaxed yowls out of a cat in her arms, even while juggling a handful of balls. An enthusiastic nonsense song came out of her mouth.

Life's a roll of the dice
Roll them day after day
And it's always snake eyes
Someone said   luck is fair
Nothing changes til the day you die
Laugh or cry, it's all the same
Snake eyes come up again today
Oh   snake eyes   snake eyes!
Show me a duodecuple tomorrow!

Guild Girl listened to the song as they walked by, then observed her companion.

"What's your roll today, Mr. Goblin Slayer?"

"I don't know," he said. "Not yet."

"Hm…" Guild Girl tapped a finger thoughtfully against her lips. Uh-huh. Right.

"You went on a date with one girl in the morning, and another in the afternoon." She pursed her lips at the slightly uncouth sound of it. "I think your luck's pretty good, don't you?"

"Is it?"

"Uh-huh."

"Is it, now?"

"It sure is."

Goblin Slayer's throat thrummed a noncommittal *hmm*. It wasn't clear if he took her point or not.

Sheesh…

Anyone else who acted this way would seem infuriatingly indecisive.

But that wasn't the kind of person he was.

If he were some playboy adventurer, she never would have invited him out like this.

"Sheesh…"

She deliberately repeated her annoyance aloud, but in the furor of the crowd, it didn't reach him.

Goblin Slayer, for his part, surveyed the performers' street.

He glanced at one act where incompetent knife throwing was supposed to elicit laughter. But he lost interest immediately and moved on to the next thing.

That next thing was a man in an overcoat.

His entire body was covered in cloth, and he made broad, strange movements with his arms…

"Oh…!"

In the next instant, a tiny dragon appeared in his upturned palm.

No sooner had Guild Girl let out a sound of amazement than the dragon was enclosed in an egg. The man covered the egg with both hands, and it grew to become a dove. The bird flew out of his hands, but his fingers sparkled and the bird turned into a cloud of blue smoke.

The man pulled on the smoke as if on a rope, nimbly shifting it into a longsword. He held the weapon up with a flourish before inserting it into his open mouth.

Guild Girl was more than happy to applaud his sleight of hand.

"That's amazing, isn't it? I didn't know anyone was so good at that."

"I see," Goblin Slayer said, his eyes never leaving the magician.

Guild Girl was a little confused, given that he hadn't seemed remotely surprised by any of the tricks.

Well, it wasn't exactly confusion—it caught her attention in a way, piqued her curiosity.

At work, she couldn't have asked him too much about it.

But happily, this was a private moment between them. She seized her chance.

"Do you like shows like that?"

"Yes." Goblin Slayer nodded and pointed to the man, whose fingers were still slightly smoky. "He distracts us with his gestures, then executes his tricks."

"They say that's the basics in sleight of hand."

"Yes. And when the audience realizes the gestures are just for show, then you make those motions the key to your next trick," Goblin Slayer said. "It's a psychological tactic, and good training."

Then he shook his helmet and looked at her. His tone was blunt as ever. But...

"...I was taken in."

Gosh, this man...

Guild Girl gave a small sigh.

He was serious, stubborn, strange, and socially awkward.

She had understood all this about him as long as they had known each other.

That was to say, for five years, ever since she had come to this town as a newly minted employee at eighteen.

But Guild Girl knew him only as an adventurer.

She did not yet know what lay beneath, or behind, that persona—his genuine self.

But the same was true for him.

She had always acted the proper receptionist with him.

"Umm, so now..."

A psychological tactic. That's what he'd said. *Okay, then. I'll show him some tactics of my own.*

"...There's somewhere I'd like to go. Is that okay?"

§

It was like the eye of a storm.

As hectic as the town was, this building alone was cloaked in silence.

The Adventurers Guild.

On such a bright, festive day, there was no one here to file a quest, nor any adventurers to take them.

Guild Girl unlocked the front door, ushering Goblin Slayer inside.

"You can make yourself comfortable. I'll be with you in just a minute."

"I see."

Their voices echoed in a space normally so loud it was hard to hear.

It was impressive how lonely the building seemed with no occupants.

Goblin Slayer had been in any number of abandoned ruins, but he had never experienced this before. Of course, ruins rarely stayed quiet for very long after he showed up...

"Hmm..."

The silhouette of a bench stretched out in the dim interior, and his own shadow danced up the wall as he walked.

Caught between the silence and the shadows, he felt like a ghost.

Goblin Slayer did what he always did—he went over to check the board.

Urgent quests had all been cleared away in anticipation of the festival. The pieces of paper left over were all noncritical adventures.

Clearing rats out of the sewers. Collecting herbs. Getting rid of a Monshroom in the mountains.

Gathering antique items for a curio collector. Patrolling the roads. Confirming the bloodline of the illegitimate child of a noble house.

Exploring unexplored ruins. Escorting a merchant caravan...

"Hrm."

Goblin Slayer skimmed everything again, just to be sure.

But, no. No goblin-slaying quests.

"..."

"Uhhh, ah, there you are. I'm ready now."

He turned around at her call, still pursuing his train of thought.

Guild Girl was waving at him from the reception area—she seemed to be holding a key of some kind.

"Come here, over here! Okay, let's go!"

And then she ducked behind the reception counter, leaving Goblin Slayer where he was.

With a final backward glance at the board, he readily followed her.

He had been affiliated with this Guild for five years, but he had never been in the employees' area.

"Is this allowed?" he asked, to which Guild Girl lightly replied, "No," as she peeked back at him.

"That's why this is just between us. Don't tell anyone, okay?"

She stuck out her tongue teasingly, and Goblin Slayer nodded.

"Okay."

"Really? I'll be unhappy if you're lying."

"Yes, really."

"I believe you, then."

She spun again, her braid bouncing in the air. Goblin Slayer trailed her deeper inside.

He heard an unfamiliar sound—Guild Girl humming. He didn't recognize the song.

At last, still in high spirits, she stood before an old door, working the key noisily in the lock.

Beyond it was a steep, weathered spiral staircase.

"It's up here. Let's go!"

"I see."

The staircase did not groan when Guild Girl stepped on it, but it did when Goblin Slayer began to climb. From the creaking of footsteps alone, one would have assumed just a single person was there.

"Oh, thank goodness!" Guild Girl said, putting a hand to her chest and straightening up. "If it had creaked under my weight, I wouldn't have been able to stand back up from the shock!"

"Is that so?"

"Sure. Girls are pretty concerned about these things."

"Is that so?"

Uh-huh, she nodded.

She glanced back over her shoulder and teased, "Would it have been better if I had worn a skirt, Mr. Goblin Slayer?"

He shook his head and said, "Keep your eyes ahead. You don't want to trip and fall."

"Aww, but you're here to catch me."

"Even so."

"All right…"

She sounded quite cheerful, though he wasn't sure what she was enjoying so much.

Soon they arrived at the pinnacle of the spiral. There they found another old door.

"Hang on a moment," Guild Girl said, using a rusty key to unlock it. "This is where I wanted to bring you."

"…Me?"

"Yes— Go ahead."

She opened the door.

The moment she did so, a draft rushed out, and his vision was filled with gold.

Mountains of treasure, jewels, enough to bewilder the senses—no.

It was the world itself, reflecting the deepening light of the sun.

Mountains, rivers, hills full of daisies, forests and farms. The town, the temple, the plaza. Everything.

This was the Guild's watchtower, and from it one could look out over everything at once in any direction.

However high, however far, it was visible from here.

Crowds bustling, musicians playing. Laughter. A song. Everything reached the tower.

If the Guild Hall was the eye of the storm, this was a place for viewing the storm itself.

Lively and joyous, a day beautiful enough to celebrate.

And Goblin Slayer stood at its very heart.

"...How is it? Surprised?"

Guild Girl stood at the railing, running her hands along it. She peeked at his helmet, but couldn't see anything.

But—she believed—there was no one easier to understand than he.

It didn't require much thought to understand his goal as he went around town.

"You were patrolling, weren't you?"

Through the streets, checking the sewers, watching the rivers for any sign of goblins at all.

That was who this person was.

So surely, if he saw everything from the guard tower, he might have...

"...Relaxed a little?"

"No..." Goblin Slayer slowly shook his head at Guild Girl's question. "I wonder, though."

He let out a breath softly.

"Is that right?" she murmured, and leaned on the railing.

Her braid danced in the wind. She didn't look at him.

"Even though you've worked so hard to slay all those goblins?"

"All the more reason."

The light grew dim. The sun was going down, sinking into the horizon. Even the most beautiful days had to end.

"…"
"…"

In its place, twin moons rose alongside a thin purple mist. The sky was full of stars—cold, sharp pinpoints of light.

The town was daubed in black, so quiet it seemed everyone was holding their breath.

The wind nipped at the two of them in the guard tower with a mournful sound.

Autumn, after all, was the prelude to winter.

They could already see their breath fogging.

And then suddenly, she whispered.

"Look, it's starting!"

The gold vanished, and the pair sank into shadows.

Then, a light.

§

One.

Two.

Three.

Four.

Five.

Finally, too many to count.

The little lanterns glittered like stars reflected in a river. Through the darkened town they shone, blinking, wavering, shining.

Finally, the warm red lights began floating into the sky like fireflies.

Like snow falling in reverse, they drifted, danced up to the heavens.

"Sky lanterns."

"Yes. I thought they would be beautiful from here." Guild Girl's response to Goblin Slayer's two words sounded rather self-satisfied. "Since I was finally going to be able to do this, I wanted to invite you along."

"…I see."

Goblin Slayer gazed at the town and exhaled quietly.

The golden spray of twilight was long gone, and in the orange glow of the candles the town was incomparably beautiful.

It was filled with the creations of humans.

Houses and buildings made of stone, the clothing of the people in the streets, their laughter rising up.

They lit the candles in their lanterns, the paper inflating before carrying the specks of light into the sky.

Goblin Slayer's gaze followed their ascent from the town below up into the night air.

He knew warm air rose, and that was why the lanterns flew. That was all. No magic and no miracles involved. Eventually, the flame would go out and the lanterns would drift back to earth.

"Mr. Goblin Slayer, do you—?"

Guild Girl opened her mouth to say something, but at that moment—

Riiing.

A bell sounded, rippling through the silence of the night.

If the lanterns were stars in a stream, this was the burble of the water.

Riiing, riiing, riiing, riiing.

The sound repeated in a set rhythm, a sacred ritual to purify the area.

Guild Girl searched for the source. It came from the plaza, where a crowd of lanterns was rising into the air.

People were packed into the square, sitting around a round stage.

She spotted a familiar spear and pointy hat in the throng and giggled.

Oh, is it that time already?

Beautiful days, festival days, celebration days. These days also belonged to the gods.

They were days of thanksgiving for the harvest and a fruitful autumn, as well as supplication for safe passage through the winter.

Petitions they made, naturally, to the all-compassionate Earth Mother.

Soon, someone appeared in the square amid the bonfires to embody those hopes.

A young woman dressed all in white emerged gracefully—a shrine maiden. No...

"O gods who gather at the table of the stars..."

It was Priestess.

She was dressed very differently. Her outfit resembled some form of battle attire, yet showed a remarkable amount of skin for that.

Her shoulders and cleavage, her midriff and back, her thighs, all showed pure and pale skin.

"…by the pips of the dice of fate and chance…"

Her blush suggested she was embarrassed to be seen this way, but nonetheless she twirled her flail modeled after a sacred relic.

The Earth Mother was the goddess of abundance, the ruler of love, and even sometimes a deity of war.

And these were the vestments of her priestess.

So in truth, there was nothing to be ashamed about.

"O Earth Mother, we beseech you…"

Priestess waved the great flail with both hands, the flames reflecting in the beads of sweat on her face.

Every time the relic, originally a tool of the harvest, cut through the air, it left white trails and the ringing of a bell.

A dance of the gods, for the gods, and to the gods. A hallowed display.

"As you will, be it my will…"

Goblin Slayer remembered her muttering, *I've been practicing.*

She'd talked about her new equipment. And she had been in such a hurry to go to the workshop.

She must have been training so she could wield that flail and gone to the shop to prepare that outfit.

He finally understood his elf companion's impish smile.

"I offer this body, tirelessly, unhesitatingly…"

Her prayer rang out through the square, past the houses, to the guard tower.

He was sure the gods could hear her where they reposed in heaven.

The hope was that their dice might roll even a bit more favorably.

Oh   snake eyes   snake eyes!

Show me a duodecuple tomorrow!

Where had he heard those words?

"We offer you this prayer…"

She wasn't possessed, exactly—but she brought the pantheon closer.

Of course, if she had truly used the Call God miracle, surely her mortal soul could not have endured.

But even in imitation of the miracle, it took only a gesture, a breath, a sound, to make the grounds seem holy.

Night did not belong to people. It belonged to monsters and chaos. And goblins.

"O great, O eternal, O vast, O deep love…"

She took a great dancing step and her garments swirled, revealing her hips.

Her heightened breath fogged, and droplets of sweat flew off her.

Her eyes teared; her lips trembled. Her small chest heaved with every breath.

Yet she exuded no eroticism, only sanctity.

"And let it be thus upon your board…"

"…I have never relaxed," Goblin Slayer whispered as he followed her form with his eyes.

"Wha…?"

The words came out of the blue. Guild Girl didn't know whether she was more surprised or confused.

It took her a moment to realize he was answering her earlier question.

"No matter how much I do, no matter how many I kill. All I gain is a chance to win." No matter how much his companions and friends supported him, encouraged him, and fought alongside him. "And a chance for victory is not victory."

There was no way it could be.

The specter of defeat was ever present. He could never flee from the shadow that had created him.

Certainly not when that shadow had a concrete form and could strike at him.

"That's why I did not make a lantern."

To prepare. To be ready against the goblins. To fight.

To hedge against that last .01 percent when he was 99.99 percent sure he could win.

He was determined that for all this, he could not spare his attention for anything else.

He knew.

He knew that what carried the flying lanterns to the sky was just a natural phenomenon. That when the candles burned out, they would fall to the earth as nothing more than trash.

Goblin Slayer knew this.

But...

"The sky lanterns guide the souls of the dead," he whispered with just a hint of regret. "I wonder if they were able to return safely."

Who could he have been talking about? Or what? How did he feel right then?

Guild Girl couldn't tell. She didn't know.

But even so she said, "I'm sure they did," and smiled.

At the same moment:

"May no ill upset the scales of order and chaos in heaven. May all be well."

Priestess tossed her hair as she lifted her eyes to the sky, offering a prayer from earth to heaven.

She chanted with all her might, her pale throat glistening with effort. Someone swallowed audibly at her beauty.

Then she intoned a supplication supposedly on behalf of many believers—those who had words.

*   *   *

"Bless the protector of the night, bring him happiness."

But she spoke only to one.

"I pray to the distant sky, I offer my petition…"

She let out a breath. It rippled through the silence.

"…Look." Guild Girl was smiling at Goblin Slayer with just a touch of surprise. "The gods are appreciating…all your hard work."

And indeed they were.

If he had not rescued Priestess in that cave, this scene would never have been. Everyone here in the town, celebrating the festival. All because he helped that girl and held off the goblin horde with her and their companions.

Was it fate or chance? That depended on the roll of the gods' dice.

Though perhaps those on the board could not imagine it…

Guild Girl didn't care which it was. Because whatever the cause, it had led her to him.

She didn't know what had brought him to become an adventurer—to become Goblin Slayer.

But she knew the five years that had led up to this point, everything he had been through in that time. He was here to protect villages, people, cities—anyone.

Just look around him.

She couldn't believe—it was ridiculous she hadn't noticed.

Goblin Slayer was not bitter. He was not sad.

She—she was the one who could barely stand it.

Guild Girl trembled with humiliation at her own selfishness.

That night, at that moment, he'd had Priestess, and High Elf Archer, and Cow Girl, too.

And even though she'd known that, she had tried to get the jump on all of them, and she hated her shameful behavior.

She hated how she had avoided them until the festival, not knowing what she would say to them.

But—but.

She was waiting. She was here.

She was supporting him, cheering him on.

She wanted him to see.

To notice.

To understand.

Her. Other things. Everyone who wasn't a goblin. Anyone at all.

She had nothing resembling the courage she needed to put any of this into words.

But now that she had managed to spend half a day with him, she wondered if anything had come of it.

Did he see me?

Did he see anyone?

Did he think about anything besides goblins?

"I'm sure…sure they were able to come home safely."

There was so much light, after all. It must be true. They couldn't have lost their way.

That faith had inspired Guild Girl's words. As ever, she hid her innermost thoughts behind her smile.

At her reassurance, he let out a faint sound, barely a word.

"…Yes."

In the end, that was all Goblin Slayer said, and then he nodded.

§

The end of the ritual marked conclusion of the festival and its blessed day.

The bonfires burned low as people trickled out of the square, just a few flames left to lick at the night skies.

The pair wandered back down the stairs, returning from the guard tower to the ground.

The sun was gone completely, leaving the Guild Hall dark.

Though she normally could have found her way around in these circumstances, today was not normal.

"Oop—oh! Whoops…"

"Be careful."

Guild Girl stumbled and caught onto Goblin Slayer's arm.

Her heart jumped at the strength in it.

She was glad it was dark. She didn't especially want him to see her face at that moment. Though she couldn't hide the catch in her voice.

"Oh, I-I'm sorry…"

"No," Goblin Slayer said, shaking his head. "It wasn't…bad."

"Wha…?"

"I mean today."

"Oh…"

"From morning until night… So this is what a 'day off' is like."

Her heart leaped again.

She felt a bit mercenary—how could she not? But she couldn't ignore the joy that overrode the calculating side of her nature.

"O-oh, no, th-think nothing of it. I-if you enjoyed today, that's wonderful."

"I see."

All the more reason she hurried toward the door, disentangling her arm from his.

The two of them were alone in the dark together. That was where this nervousness came from.

When they got outside, she was sure the feeling would change. That she would breathe easier.

With that in mind, she took the doorknob…

"…What?"

She cocked her head when it didn't turn.

"What's wrong?"

Goblin Slayer approached at a perfectly normal pace despite the darkness.

"Am I remembering wrong?" she was saying, still bewildered. "No… I didn't lock the door. But…"

It's locked.

The words began to form, not quite on her lips, when Goblin Slayer moved.

He grabbed Guild Girl around the waist and dove to the ground.

"Whaa?!"

He knocked over a table to shield them.

She fell on her backside, and a blade buried itself in the tabletop at almost the same moment.

"O-ow! Wh-what's going on?!"

"Stay close to the wall. Watch your back and keep quiet."

Goblin Slayer freed his sword from its scabbard as he whispered his commands.

Staying low, he slowly crawled sideways from behind their cover, maintaining his distance.

He pulled the knife from the tabletop and saw how it glinted starkly in the night. Then he set off after their attacker.

Far be it from Goblin Slayer to let them escape.

A small shape—a small man, about half the size of a human—scuttled through the darkness.

"A goblin?"

The only answer was a jeering hiss that smelled faintly of blood.

Then the attacker leaped.

He held a knife in a reverse grip, bringing it down like a predator's fang.

Goblin Slayer brought up his shield to defend. There was a dull sound. A spray of liquid.

"Coated in poison."

The slimy secretion rained on his helmet. But he had his visor. It would not blind him.

The enemy broke contact and landed on the ground, taking advantage of the distance that opened up for a lightning fast second strike.

Goblin Slayer deflected the oncoming blows with his shield and swiped with his sword, hoping to catch his attacker in the abdomen.

Sparks danced, lighting up the darkness.

The attacker had a knife in his left hand as well, using it to sweep aside Goblin Slayer's blade.

His technique was refined, the assailant evidently an experienced hand.

"You seem most unlike a goblin."

"G-Goblin Slayer…!" cried Guild Girl.

"There is no problem."

She heard a creaking sound—the assailant gnashing his teeth, perhaps?

Guild Girl's eyes were adjusting to the darkness, but the battling forms were still indistinct.

The attacker wore leather armor and protection around his abdomen. The cloth around it was light black, and so was his face…

"No…a dark elf?!"

Her shout served as a signal.

The attacker swung the knife in his left hand fast enough to cut the air itself and followed up immediately with something in his right.

Dazzling sparks burst from Goblin Slayer's shield as he blocked the small blade three times.

Darts!

The brief illumination also allowed her to see the true attack behind the feint.

"Hrr…!"

The volley forced Goblin Slayer backward in a sort of half somersault.

He tumbled into the table with a spectacular crash, sending dust up into the dark air.

"Oh, ah, G-Goblin Slayer…?"

There was no answer.

Even in silhouette, she could see the numerous darts sticking out of his armor.

It was too much.

"No…"

"Yes!" A great shout drowned out her pained whisper. It came, obviously, from the enemy, who bellowed with a spray of spittle, "I did it! I did it! Hya-ha-ha-ha! Because of him—it's all because of him!"

He cackled horribly as he jumped up and down, clapping his hands.

He stumbled over to Goblin Slayer and gave him a kick for good measure.

"Silver-ranked, pfft! Easy prey and a bit of luck, that's all he had!"

Another kick. A third, then a fourth.

Goblin Slayer's head bobbed each time the crude boot connected. The visor of his grimy helmet clattered awfully as he flopped like a cheap doll.

It was unbearable to watch.

Until just minutes ago, they had been talking together, walking together.

"S-stop it…"

She could only whisper, so quietly no one could have heard.

But now something was welling up in her heart.

"I said, stop it!"

"Serves him right for keeping all the girls for himself." The assailant spun, his glinting eye fixed on Guild Girl. She made a fist in front of her chest. "And he was on such close terms with a Guild employee, no less. Not so righteous as he pretended to be, I think!"

Should she have kept silent? No. It had to be said.

She felt regret, but also a resolve that overcame it. Of course. No one had the right to kick him like that.

The poison dribbled from the dagger with a revolting color.

Should she shout again, call someone? No… Even if she did, it would be too late.

"!"

If nothing else, she would not avert her eyes.

Her intense glare only seemed to anger the attacker more.

"Don't think I'll let you off easy…!"

"Is that so?"

The voice was cold as wind from the depths of a well.

"___"

"What? Gargh…!"

Guild Girl's eyes went wide, and the assailant could only manage a muffled choke.

Goblin Slayer alone moved.

He rose like a specter, still riddled with darts. His sword—

His sword was buried in the attacker's viscera, having neatly found a gap in the opponent's leather armor.

He tore violently through the man's innards, causing their former aggressor to cough and choke.

The body fell backward, twitching, losing blood and strength.

"Hmph."

Goblin Slayer snorted, bracing his foot against the bloodied form as he pulled his sword out.

The attacker gave one last raw cough, then lay still.

"Go—" Guild Girl's voice trembled. "Goblin Slayer…?"

"Yes?"

"Are you okay?! Are you hurt?!"

"I wear chain mail under my leather armor," he said matter-of-factly, gently pushing away Guild Girl as she frantically tried to come close. "A simple dart can't penetrate it."

He grabbed the barbs and pulled them out of his armor. The tips were drenched in something—presumably the same fluid that had coated the dagger.

Goblin Slayer said disinterestedly, "He was a quick one. With my skill, I could not have beaten him."

That meant that—to him, at least—the obvious solution had been a sneak attack. He could not win in a fair fight, so he didn't engage in one.

But Guild Girl did not entirely sympathize with this perspective.

"I-I thought you...were dead......!"

Even as she spoke, tears beaded in her eyes and ran down her cheeks.

Once they had started, there was no stopping them. Confronted with the sobbing girl, Goblin Slayer could muster only, "Hrk..." He shook the blood off his sword to distract himself. "I'm sorry."

"If... If you have to apologize...you shouldn't...do it to begin with...!"

"...I won't."

Goblin Slayer nodded, and then with the tip of his sword he slid off the attacker's mask.

"*Sniff...* Is...? Is he a dark elf?"

"That I don't know."

Guild Girl raised her head, still sniffling.

Dark elves were among the peoples who had words, also known as Players. They shared the same roots as other elves, but aligned them-selves with chaos.

It could not be assumed that they were all Non-Players, those unpraying beings, because from time to time, a dark elf would return to the side of order.

With just a handful of exceptions, most dark elves were evil and rev-eled in defying law and order.

Noboru Kannatuki

They had pointed ears like other elves, but light black skin.

She had heard they were usually tall, like their forest dwelling cousins, but the body on the floor hadn't grown so well.

"But this is a rhea."

"Wha…?"

Guild Girl gasped as she took another look at the corpse.

The face was black and grimy, but she had a distant memory of it.

And why not? Why else would he cover his face when he attacked?

Goblin Slayer used the heel of his boot to wipe the corpse's face clean.

"Oh! That's…!" Guild Girl put a hand to her mouth. She *did* recognize him. "He's the one we accused of wrongdoing in that interview…!"

The features were twisted with hatred and bitterness and desire for revenge…but it was undoubtedly Rhea Scout.

An adventurer they had interviewed for promotion. The man who had quietly hoarded rewards and treasures for himself and hid them from his party members.

The interviewers had all but exiled him— Had he come back? Or had he been in town ever since?

Goblin Slayer stared at the rhea's face.

"I believe I remember him."

"Yeah. You sat in on our interview with him. That's why—"

"No." Goblin Slayer shook his head. "When I was eating at the tavern, he was whispering with another person. I saw him watching me at the Guild Hall before that, too."

"You mean…"

"But if he had meant to target me alone, he wouldn't have needed such strange clothing."

Goblin Slayer grunted.

So many possibilities, so many choices—he couldn't seem to decide what exactly he should do.

But there was only one conclusion to pursue, one warning to heed.

"The goblins may be on the move."

With that declaration, Goblin Slayer pounded his sword into its sheath.

"I'm going. Can you stand?"

"Oh, um..."

Guild Girl didn't quite know where to look. She was kneeling as if her legs were weak, but she was able to move.

But if she said she couldn't, would he stay? Would it be better if he did?

"I... I'm fine."

She mustered everything she had to say this, then reached out and put a hand on the table.

Goblin Slayer collected the darts in the rhea's mask, then stuffed them in his pouch. He wiped the poisoned dagger's blade and belted it on.

After a quick check of his equipment, he inspected where the darts had hit him. He decided there was no problem.

"In that case, please take care of things here."

Nodding, Guild Girl used the table as support to unsteadily rise to her feet.

What had happened? What was happening? She didn't know. How could she know?

The day of celebration was over. Her day of happiness was gone.

"...I just, I mean, I don't... I don't understand all of this, myself..."

Well then. She would just have to go back to being the Guild receptionist, treating him like another adventurer.

"B-but whatever it is, please do your best!"

She put the biggest smile she could manage on her face, and Goblin Slayer answered with just two words:

"I will."

Of the Gods' Creating a New Scenario

Now she'd done it.

Yes, even the sweet-hearted goddess Illusion could make a mistake.

She had found a vibrant young girl living in a village.

She had noticed that this girl had feelings—though one-sided—for a boy who was ill.

She prepared story markers to lead her to an herb that would cure the illness.

She guided hale and trustworthy allies to the girl to aid her.

The caves and monsters in the girl's path she made simple enough to overcome.

All was set. All was perfect. She was ready to oversee the girl's brilliant adventure.

Then came the moment of truth. She flung the dice as hard as she could...

But it morphed into an awful thing.

Unhappily, unluckily, the girl's swords and spells missed by a mile.

The monsters, who should have been no hindrance at all, landed crushing blows and wiped the girl and her party out.

Not even the gods know if this world is ruled by fate or chance.

Thus, the dice alone are absolute. They cannot be rerolled.

Of course, there is nothing to say that a second roll would come out any better than the first. But be that as it may.

The goddess Illusion lost the adventurers she had watched over so caringly, so lovingly.

It was a common enough story. Most unfortunate. But it was done, and there was no undoing it.

The poor young woman's exploit ended there. It was time to ready the next adventurer.

But before that, the goddess went to her bed, buried herself in the blankets, and wept into her pillow.

She would probably be sniffling away for some time before she got over the loss of this adventurer—just like with all the others.

The trouble was the god Truth.

This god cast his eye upon the accursed thing in the deepest reaches of the dungeon, the thing the girl had never been able to obtain.

Illusion was otherwise occupied, and if she wasn't going to use it, why shouldn't he?

This was his chance to create a trial that would really give those adventurers something to chew on.

A Demon Lord, a Dark God, or some yet unknown ancient threat revived.

Never-before-seen traps, unsolvable labyrinths, fearsome monsters, strange quest givers, betrayal, intrigue!

The more experienced the adventurer, the less likely they were to accept a quest without scrutinizing it closely.

By the time Illusion realized what Truth had so gleefully prepared, things were already well under way.

She could hardly order him to stop now, but events seemed headed for a terrible conclusion.

Now, what would Illusion do…?

CHAPTER 5

A Scenario Overturned

"Whoa, what's with him?"

"Has anyone ever seen such a dirty adventurer?"

"Hey, isn't that Goblin Slayer?"

"Goblin Slayer?"

"They say he specializes in slaying goblins."

"So is that getup part of his goblin slaying strategy?"

"I guess. He *is* Goblin Slayer."

"Goblin Slayer...huh."

"Heeeeyyy! Watch out for goblins!"

Goblin Slayer ran doggedly through the crowd, weaving among citizens still under the festival's thrall.

He wore his grimy leather armor and cheap-looking helmet, carried his sword of a strange length, and had his round shield strapped to his arm.

Even a brand-new adventurer would have had better equipment, but his form quickly disappeared into the throng.

He received some strange looks, but no unknowing ones.

The Guild Hall was at the entrance to the town, just beside the town gate. Having left Guild Girl behind, he made a beeline for that gate, and beyond it...

"Goblin Slayer, sir!" He heard a voice like a tinkling bell behind him.

He didn't need to turn around. He already recognized its owner.

"You've come."

"Yes, sir! I received a handout...an oracle!"

It was Priestess, clutching her staff—no, her flail—with both hands.

She was still dressed in her scant ritual outfit as she rushed up, her breath coming in labored gulps.

So it was she, and not Goblin Slayer, who attracted the most stares.

She managed a serious expression even as she flushed with embarrassment.

"It told me to find you... Um, what...?"

"Goblins, I'm sure."

As the pair passed through the town gate, a shadow approached them soundlessly from the side.

That clear voice. That slim figure. High Elf Archer's ears bounced, and her eyes narrowed like a cat.

"If Orcbolg's running, what else could it be?"

"Indubitably, indubitably."

"Beard-cutter here isn't exactly hard to fathom."

Two more shadows followed her.

The towering Lizard Priest joined his hands together in a strange gesture, while Dwarf Shaman stroked his beard merrily.

Each of them was already prepared with whatever equipment they thought best for battle.

"...Hrm."

Goblin Slayer grunted and stood still.

He looked at each of them. They could not see his expression behind his helmet.

"You want to know why we're all here, even though you didn't call us." His thoughts were hidden, but not hard to guess. High Elf Archer explained: "Don't underestimate an elf's ears." She gave hers a self-congratulatory flick. "You think I can't hear a couple guys whispering in a tavern? Or spread the word?" She held up her dainty pointer finger, making a circle in the air. "One adventure! With me—with everyone. That's our price for helping you."

"...I see."

Goblin Slayer nodded brusquely, and High Elf Archer's ears bobbed.

"Hey, is that—is that all?! Aren't you going to thank us or praise us or anything?"

"No..." He had a moment of hesitation. As though even he was not quite sure what to do.

Goblin Slayer groped for words, then said, without emotion but unmistakably:

"...Thanks. For helping."

"No worries," Priestess said with a little giggle she couldn't hold back. Still clasping her flail, her gaze worked its way up his frame. "We're your friends, aren't we?"

"I see." Goblin Slayer nodded. "...Yes, you are."

At that, the four adventurers exchanged glances and smiled broadly. Whatever they were about to get themselves into, they were unconcerned. After all, the special day had ended. This would be just another regular day. For an adventurer, each new day meant a new adventure.

"You may tell us to pay you no mind, girl, but it's not easy to ignore that costume of yours," Dwarf Shaman teased, stroking his beard and smirking.

"Dirty old man," High Elf Archer complained. Priestess waved her hands frantically.

"Um! Oh! Uh! I! It's because of the ritual... I didn't have time to change...!"

"I find it most flattering on you." Lizard Priest rolled his eyes and laughed with open jaws. "What do you think, milord Goblin Slayer?"

Goblin Slayer's response was detached.

"Not bad."

"Gwaaah?!"

Priestess was not the only one who was surprised. As she stood there blushing furiously, Lizard Priest stuck out his tongue, as if unsure how to deal with the answer to his own question. High Elf Archer began to seriously worry about Goblin Slayer's health, and even Dwarf Shaman froze.

Goblin Slayer gazed at the party, then clarified.

"I am referring to our circumstances."

Everyone sighed. Priestess puffed out her cheeks and said nothing.

"...Looks like a storm's coming."

Goblin Slayer nodded at High Elf Archer's whisper, then launched into an explanation.

"From the Guild watchtower I saw shadows in every direction. Most likely goblins are coming."

"What?!" Dwarf Shaman's eyes were wide. He nearly spat out his swig of wine, then hurriedly swallowed it. "That's worrisome, that is. That last horde took more than a little mopping up."

"Mm. Could we not call on the aid of other adventurers as we did then?" asked Lizard Priest.

"No…" He cut himself off, then gazed back toward town.

The celebration, the festival, they were over now. People were returning to their homes. A few were still weaving drunkenly, loath to let the fun end.

People of all races and jobs lived here, and similarly diverse adventurers did, too.

Goblin Slayer thought.

He thought of Heavy Warrior. Of Female Knight.

He thought of Scout Boy and Druid Girl, of Rookie Warrior and Apprentice Priestess.

And finally, he thought of Spearman and Witch.

"…This time…"

Upon this calm reflection, Goblin Slayer shook his head slowly.

He knew now how much courage it took simply to speak.

Was there anything more terrifying in all the world than trusting everything to luck?

He considered Priestess from behind his visor. She was visibly frightened, but facing forward.

She had said before that luck had nothing to do with anything.

Goblin Slayer made a fist.

"…I believe our strength will be sufficient."

"But Beard-cutter," Dwarf Shaman said, checking the catalysts in his bag, "if there's too many of them… Well, there were a lot of them last time. We couldn't have done it alone."

"Of course not," Goblin Slayer said evenly. "No one person can face down a goblin army on an open field."

"So you think this time will be different?"

"Our enemy is divided. There are only a few in each unit, and they are not well coordinated. And I have already made some preparations."

High Elf Archer glanced at him, surprised he could be so calm.

"Preparations? How exactly did you know these goblins were coming, Orcbolg?"

"Because if I knew a nest of goblins would be drunk from celebrating, I'd attack it."

"...Hmph. I see."

His answer could not have been more direct.

"Hurry. I'll explain the rest while we move."

Goblin Slayer set off even as he spoke, and the others joined him.

They left the main road, flitting among the trees and vegetation along forest footpaths.

Each of them trailed him closely as he set a pace worthy of Ranger.

After all, if an adventurer couldn't follow a scout through a labyrinth of ruins, that would be the end.

"Did you know there have not been many goblin-slaying quests lately?"

"I guess I didn't. But so what?" High Elf Archer ran lightly alongside, her ears bouncing. She loped along slowly enough that the others could keep up. Priestess had never been very athletic, and lizardmen and dwarves were not known for speed.

"They are parasites. They can't survive without stealing from others."

"Sure you—*huff, huff*—haven't just killed 'em all already?"

Goblin Slayer glanced at Dwarf Shaman, working his stubby arms and legs as hard as he could, and moderated his pace.

"Not possible."

"And why's that?"

"Because they haven't been touching the women they kidnap. If their numbers were dropping, they would prioritize reproduction."

Goblins who ignored the women they abducted were as bizarre as dragons who did not hoard gold or necromancers with no interest in corpses.

"Hrrm," Lizard Priest grunted, keeping his head low so he could speak while they ran, balancing with his tail. "Meaning...there is something or someone else providing them with their resources and causing them to abscond with those women."

"Hey, you know..." Priestess sounded like she had suddenly remembered something.

Lizard Priest, for his part, indicated the flail she was holding with his tail and asked if she wanted him to hold it for her. She smiled and refused, then spoke.

"…Those goblins we ran into were well equipped, weren't they? Armor and weapons and all…"

"If we presume those items were not simply purloined, it would mean some other entity supplied them to the goblins."

"Yes." Goblin Slayer nodded.

Like that whatever-it-was-called, the giant monster they had encountered in the ruins before.

Or the nameless eyeball creature they had found in the sewers beneath the water town.

Goblins were effectively the foot soldiers of chaos, meaning their leader might not itself be a goblin.

"I don't know who it is, and I don't care. But—" He considered the question trifling, not worth his time. "—I placed traps on the roads they prefer to use in every direction. We'll take care of the rest ourselves."

The enemy was goblins. Nothing more.

He simply kept running, his friends exchanging weary smiles behind him.

After all, if adventuring was a day's work for an adventurer…

"Goblins' numbers are their only strength. Only an amateur leader would divide them."

…then slaying goblins was a day's work for Goblin Slayer.

"And we're going to teach them that firsthand."

Far in the distance, thunder began to roll.

§

Thus the goblins arrived at the frontier town.

North of town, the fifteen goblins in the first of the bands around the town were thrilled by the chance to march at "noon."

For many months, their "commander" had insisted they curb their desires.

And no matter the reassurance that they would later be allowed to do whatever they pleased, goblins hated to be patient.

Goblins believed in never putting off till tomorrow what one could do today, at least when it came to indulging themselves. Why wait for dinner when one could have lunch?

This was not because they were too stupid to think about the future, but because they saw it as the only way to survive.

At any rate, the goblins were starving.

They were starving and bored and sick of waiting—and more than anything, they wanted some pleasures to divert them.

Attacking a town full of people sleeping off a festival's revelry sounded like just the thing, and their morale was high.

They wore a motley collection of equipment, and their footsteps were light as they walked in formation.

Night had only just fallen. To them it was dawn, so they were still somewhat tired, but soon their moment would come.

What had they to fear? What reason had they to hesitate?

"GROOBR…?"

"GROOB! GOROOBBR!"

And yet, they stopped moving.

In the moonlight that sifted through the clouds, they could see a single rope drawn across the footpath in front of them.

The goblins snickered to one another. What fools these humans were.

One of them cut the rope with a crude spear tip, and a rattling could be heard in the bushes.

They followed the sound and found a simple device of wood boards strung along the rope.

Even goblins recognized an alarm when they saw one.

What did the humans expect to gain by this? They gave it a kick and sent it flying.

"GROROBR!!"

"GOBRR!"

The advance resumed.

Their captain waved his hand, and the goblins set off at a walk, smirking to one another.

The site of the festival was not far ahead. The people had had their celebration. Now it was the goblins' turn. They forged ahead, singing a terrible dirge in their howling voices.

All without realizing that adventurers were watching them from the bushes.

"G-Goblin Slayer, sir, they disarmed your trap…!"

"Everything's fine."

"Huh?" The panicked Priestess was frankly taken aback as she looked over her shoulder at Goblin Slayer.

"That was not the trap. Merely a decoy."

"…Wha? Wh-what do we do then? At this rate…"

"Just watch. You'll see."

No sooner had he spoken than there was a low, keening sound.

Did the goblins even notice it?

It was the sound of a tight string suddenly being released.

In the next instant, something flew out of the bushes and attacked the goblin party. Sharpened stakes or spears—no, they were giant arrows.

Long, sharp, thick pieces of wood that had been shaved to the sharpest possible points.

Propelled from branches that acted as oversized bows, the missiles soared directly at the goblins.

"GROOROB?!"

"GOBR?!"

Shrieks and cries. The awful death rattles of those borne to their end on a wave of agony.

Fortunate were the goblins that expired immediately from the skewers. Others, shot through the stomach, were unable to extract the stakes and could only wait for death.

But that single volley hardly finished off the goblins, of course.

"GOORB! GOBRR!!"

The bolts had missed some completely. The survivors sent up shouts of fury and hatred, then raised their weapons and began to run.

They never entirely decided whether they were running away or pushing ahead, because Goblin Slayer and Lizard Priest jumped out of the bushes and descended upon the goblins with their swords.

"The trap seems to have benefited from my test firing."

"Indeed! And now behold! Take pride in my deeds, O my ancestors!"

The goblins screamed as their hearts were skewered, their throats torn out, their skulls crushed, and their innards scattered.

©Noboru Kannatuki

Amid the shouts could be heard the unique, high-pitched prayer of Lizard Priest, echoing in the night. The destruction of heresy was his joy as much as his mission.

That was to say, his motivation was different from Goblin Slayer's, but their goals were the same.

Compared to the calm, methodical Goblin Slayer, Lizard Priest's fighting style was brimming with exultation.

"Thirteen—ahem, or rather, fourteen!"

"No. Fifteen."

The fight lasted only moments, the goblins ending up as cruelly exposed corpses.

Perhaps it is unnecessary to say that no goblin was luckier than those who had died instantly in that first volley of oversized arrows.

"Erk... Oh..." High Elf Archer blanched a little at the sight from where she perched in the trees with her bud-tipped arrows at the ready.

She was supposed to shoot any goblins who tried to flee, but in the end that hadn't been necessary.

And yet—well, this—

"I can't count the number of times I've had to wonder what you're thinking, Orcbolg..."

"This is what I'm thinking."

"...Spare me..."

High Elf Archer leaped down from her branch, making no sound, bending no leaf or blade of grass.

She really could barely stand it, though. On any other adventure, this would have been beyond the pale.

"That trap is off-limits for anything but goblin slaying!"

"Hrk..."

"Well, there's a time and place for everything," offered Dwarf Shaman, who had been waiting quietly in the rear with Priestess in the interest of conserving his spells. He stroked his beard with a thoughtful mutter, inspecting the contraption that had just wreaked such destruction.

The rope that appeared to be an alarm had been connected to a thick branch nearby. The branch had been bent like a bow with the stakes sharpened like javelins on top of it. When the rope was cut, the stakes came flying—a primitive ballista.

"A simple trap. But rather effective for all that."

"It was originally for hunting game."

Goblin Slayer's sword had now endured both this battle and the fight at the Guild Hall, and he unhesitatingly threw it away.

"Where did you learn of it?"

"From my older sister," he said briefly, scavenging through the bodies. "My father was a hunter. She learned it from him."

He picked up the best blade he could find, checked the edge, and then sheathed it.

"It requires a certain knack. The goblins won't figure it out the first time they see it."

"Though it needs a proper location and time to prepare for its shortcomings. Now then, milord Goblin Slayer, what do we do next?" Lizard Priest shook the blood off his fang blade, touching the tip of his nose with his tongue.

"I have an idea." Goblin Slayer inclined his helmet slightly. "...Are you finished?"

"Oh, uh, yes!" Priestess nodded, rising from where she had been praying for the souls of the dead.

There would be much more killing to come. There was no time to bury the bodies here and now.

But Goblin Slayer never interfered with her prayers, at the very least.

"The Earth Mother's power is still strong. I doubt they'll become undead on this night."

"I see... Do you still have that handout, or whatever you called it?"

"No," Priestess said, shaking her head. "I think it must have been just for that one moment."

"I see," Goblin Slayer muttered, and nodded.

He accepted all this without a word of complaint.

Where she had risen, he now knelt at the side of a corpse, taking a goblin dagger for his own belt. He searched the creature for anything else that might be of use, then glanced at High Elf Archer.

"What's going on?"

"Let's see... Give me a minute."

She closed her eyes, her long ears trembling ever so slightly.

Even Dwarf Shaman kept his mouth shut, leaving only silence—or rather, the whistling of the wind.

Then, there was the rustling of grass, the breathing of animals. Insects buzzing and thunder rumbling. And—

"…The west. It's loudest over there, so that's probably next. The east, too."

"I see. What about the others?"

"I'm kind of worried about the hill to the south, even though it's a ways off…" Her ears fluttered confidently. She sniffed, picking up the scent in the air. "Rain is coming. The thunder's getting louder."

"Mm," Goblin Slayer grunted, then turned to Lizard Priest and said, "What do you think?"

"…The weather is on the side of our enemies tonight. Rain would be perfect for cloaking themselves." Lizard Priest tapped his nose with his tongue and let out a hiss. "We must kill all of them. If even one or two reach the town, victory is theirs."

"We'll have to hurry, then," Goblin Slayer said bluntly.

"Those storm clouds… I've got a bad feeling about them," Priestess said. It wasn't the cold that made her shoulders shake. "They have the sense of… I don't know. Chaos. Something unnatural."

"Hrm…"

Their elf, who was in tune with all natural things, and their priest-ess, who served the goddess of the land, were both anxious.

Perhaps they should assume this was a spell cast by a goblin sha-man, or by the one behind the goblin attacks.

Goblin Slayer, for his part, had never met a goblin with such power. But that was no assurance that one did not exist.

They would have to hypothesize and plan, and they would have to win.

His thoughts were interrupted when an open palm struck him hard on the back.

"What, now, no need to be so serious, Beard-cutter!" It was Dwarf Shaman. Dwarves' small stature belied their physical strength, and this one gave Goblin Slayer another slap on the back. "We're hardly even playing the same game they are! Just do what you always do."

Goblin Slayer nodded.

"…Right."

The truth was, there wasn't much time to think, anyway.

They were few, and their enemy legion.

They would have to be quick, subtle, and precise if they wanted to have any chance of victory.

It was only the presence of his party members that kept him from conceding defeat. That was something he had no inkling how to repay.

He had no idea—but if they requested an adventure, then he would go on an adventure.

Even if they forbade him from using his traps for some reason—well, he had plenty of other tactics.

"From the east and the west, is it? They're attempting a pincer attack." Goblin Slayer rose. "We're going to stop them."

§

At the risk of giving away the rest of the story, that is exactly what they did.

The thunder rumbled overhead, and the insects cried from their hidden places in the grass.

The goblins approaching through the woods from the west stopped when they saw the lights of the town.

They could see humanoid shapes.

Something was pressed up against the trees along the roadside, as though it thought it was hidden.

But the helmet was all too obvious. There was no mistaking it. This was some kind of adventurer.

The goblin leading them—not through any personal desire or ambition—made a "wait" gesture.

He pointed to a subordinate, then shoved the spear he held into the creature's hands. *Go jab that shadow.*

"GRBB."

"GOOB!"

The subordinate shook his head furiously; his leader replied with a slap in the face and a kick in the rear.

The goblin now holding the weapon shuffled fearfully closer.

There was no movement. The goblin swallowed heavily.

He hefted the crude spear and offered his best stab.

It was a good blow, by goblin standards. Certainly enough to take a person's life.

The blade struck something with a thump.

At the same moment, the silhouette tilted, then collapsed without a sound.

The goblins were simple creatures. Satisfied with the results, they set off again.

So they didn't notice until it was too late.

They didn't notice the rusty old helmet roll to the ground, revealing the face that had been chalked onto it.

It wasn't a person?

In the next instant, a weighted pulley went into action, and death came raining down on the goblins' heads.

"_____!"

"_____?!"

Death arrived in the form of sharpened stakes clustered in balls.

The balls were attached to the pulley by a string, and the force of the pulley flung them mercilessly down on their victims.

Adventurers referred to these nasty spiked balls as *Guten Tag*, popularly understood to mean "Good day—now die!"

After they had made a first pass through the goblins, the spiked balls pitched back under their own weight and speed, swinging like pendulums.

As much as they wanted to, the goblins found themselves unable to scream and failed to raise the alarm.

In fact—there was no noise at all.

"O Earth Mother, abounding in mercy, grant us peace to accept all things…"

It was, if you will, a miracle.

The wind tousled Priestess's garments while she raised her flail in stunning fashion during the spell's incantation.

Silence. Proof that the gods responded to her faithful heart.

Priestess was protected from the goblins in front of her by the Earth Mother's blessing.

But the goblins, whose ranks had been culled by the trap, were not simply scared.

They believed anyone but themselves should suffer harm, and they burned with anger over their fallen companions.

That was simply their nature.

"—!!!"

With a soundless war cry, the goblins raised primitive weapons and attempted to mob Priestess.

In moments, the maiden would surely be overrun, trampled by goblin feet.

They should have known.

No support role would take on a horde of goblins alone.

"—?!"

One of the monsters suddenly tumbled spectacularly to the ground.

What was this? They all stopped to see. An arrow protruded from the forehead of the fallen creature.

Suddenly a bud-tipped arrow blossomed from the throat of another monster, having threaded all the way through the mouth.

It brought to mind the saying that a sufficiently advanced skill was indistinguishable from magic.

Nothing exemplified that maxim as well as High Elf Archer plying her elven marksmanship. Sometimes the great poets understand even better than the ancient elves.

The arrows released not a whisper as they flew, scything through the crowd of foes.

One after another was struck down, sowing a mighty confusion— and the goblins could not endure chaos or ambush for long.

Still, the very last of them came within footsteps of Priestess—

"Take...that!"

She sounded almost relieved as she smacked the attacker soundly with her flail. As he reeled from the blow, two, then three, arrows found him... And all was still.

"Huff... Huff..."

"Nice work. I'd say that went pretty well." High Elf Archer patted Priestess on the shoulder. The younger girl was still gasping for breath, while her enemy's remains collapsed just feet away.

"Th-thank you. S-somehow, I..."

Sweat streamed down her face, yet she smiled bravely. She tried hard to remain standing.

"Sheesh." High Elf Archer laughed, stroking Priestess's head.

"Huh?"

"When someone tells you to be bait, it's okay to be a little upset about it."

"Well, I mean… I guess…" But, blinking, Priestess concluded, "It was just my role in the plan."

"You just don't care with Orcbolg, do you? He could punch you in the face and you'd forgive him."

"Ah— Ah, ha-ha-ha…"

High Elf Archer made a sound of disgust and reminded her that he'd instructed them to count the bodies.

Priestess said nothing and picked the helmet up off the ground with a strained expression.

Well used and covered in gruesome blotches, it was the same as Goblin Slayer's helmet. It was probably an old one of his that he had saved for a situation exactly like this one.

She patted the visor. *Sheesh. Really.* She smiled and murmured.

"Well, he can't be helped."

And what was that person "who couldn't be helped" doing at that moment?

He was killing goblins, of course.

§

"Hmph."

A rock whistled through the air, cracking a goblin's skull.

The creature stumbled and fell backward before vanishing into the murk.

"GOROOG?!"

Perhaps *vanishing* was the wrong word—or rather, only a human perspective. The superior night vision of goblins was perfectly capable of perceiving what had happened to their companion.

He was at the bottom of the cleft in the ground—a hole filled with sharpened spikes.

"GRRROROR!"

"GORRRB!"

The pit was merely a pit. But it was still a pit.

The goblins did not know that such traps had claimed the lives of many adventurers in many labyrinths.

But they did know better than to push ahead at random.

When the first one dropped into the hole along the footpath, the warband came to a halt.

Colored pebbles dotted the road in front of them.

Ah, markers!

The leader of the goblin party, pleased with his own perceptiveness, ordered his troops to avoid the pebbles.

The first step they took went quite well. Then the second, the third, the fourth. On the fifth step—

Another creature was swallowed up into a suddenly gaping maw.

"GOROOB?!"

"GROOROB! GOROBOB!!"

The goblins fell into a panic. There were no colored stones here.

Those pebbles had not marked anything at all. They had merely been a distraction.

The goblins were falling steadily into pits now. They couldn't advance and they couldn't retreat.

Those first steps had simply been lucky. There was no guarantee the ground would still be safe if they passed back over it.

"GROB! GOROROB!"

"GOOROBOG!!"

Soon they were at one another's throats.

It was an ugly fight. The underlings blamed the leader who had told them to forge ahead, while the leader tried to foist the blame on his followers.

Caught up in their mutual suspicion and anger, none of them realized that this was precisely the point.

That was why some of the colored stones had, in fact, marked a pit.

And Goblin Slayer was not one to give up the advantage of surprise.

More whistling stones whipped through the air, striking down one goblin after another.

The screeching, scrambling monsters tossed their spears, threw rocks, cognizant that they were fighting for their lives.

But all their projectiles were repelled by the defensive wall *he* had prepared beforehand.

"Gracious. Wouldn't our lives have been easier if we'd kept Long-Ears with us?" Dwarf Shaman growled, working stone and sling with his stubby fingers. He always carried the weapon, but magic was his forte.

"Not possible." Goblin Slayer calmly fired off a stone, muttering, "Nineteen." Then he explained, "She has less endurance. In a fight behind fortifications, it would be dangerous if any unexpected events were to occur."

"Unexpected events… Do you speak of a shaman, perchance?" Lizard Priest was gathering stones for the two of them, setting them at their feet. He poked his head out from behind the battlement.

Two to the right, several yet to the left. He indicated the numbers to Goblin Slayer with his fingers, who gave his acknowledgment.

"Correct." Goblin Slayer nodded, provoking a grumble from the dwarf.

"Well. She may have an anvil for a chest, but I suppose she is more at home leaping through the trees than crouching behind a pile of dirt."

"I admit, it bothers me," Goblin Slayer said.

"The fact that she doesn't even have enough bosom to jiggle?"

"No." As he made this flat refusal, he peeked through an opening in the battlement at the goblins, who were on the brink of routing. "Four bands of fifteen makes a total of sixty… Have you seen any superior breeds?"

"They all appear to be quite average, as far as I can tell."

"Scaly's right. Though Long-Ears might be able to pick up something else."

"No spell-casters, no champions, no lords, no meat shields. And all attacking at precisely the same moment…?" Goblin Slayer muttered. "I can only think they are toying with us."

Dwarf Shaman nodded. Not entirely without flippancy, but he was more serious than before.

"Can't just chalk this one up to goblin idiocy, can we?"

"They're stupid, but they're not fools."

"Meaning," Lizard Priest said with a swish of his tail, "their mysterious commander believes he has a chance of victory."

"We should assume so."

The last one. Goblin Slayer split its skull, counting off, "Thirty."

After making sure the corpse had fallen into the pit, he rose from behind the wall.

"We should link up with the others, then go reinforce the southern route."

"The south—that's where your farm is, isn't it?" Dwarf Shaman asked.

"Yes."

The next question came from Lizard Priest.

"Have you set traps near the farm?"

"No."

"But that's where you want to have the final confrontation?" Dwarf Shaman seemed to doubt the soundness of this plan.

"It is where they expect to launch their attack," he said. "They are wrong."

In other words.

"We will slaughter all the goblins."

That was when the first droplet descended from the heavens and onto Goblin Slayer's visor.

It would be a wet battle.

It had been a long and difficult battle.

But now five—no, six—mangled corpses lay before him.

New equipment, still just recognizable for what it was, was the only remaining testament to its former owners.

The girls had opposed him tenaciously, but with enough of a beating from his goblins…

Perhaps I should have left them alive?

He shook his head lightly, dismissing the thought as soon as it came to him. Useless speculation.

If the girl in the front lines had not taken that club to the face, shattering her lovely forehead, he would probably be dead instead of her.

But by fate or by chance, the gods had granted him a critical hit.

It would not be an exaggeration to say that it determined the course of the fight.

The air was humid, thick with the sweet stench of rotting flesh, and buffeted by a piercing cold. He savored all of it.

His eyes functioned as well in this dimness as they did in daylight. The grumbling goblins in front of him he found at once ridiculous and lovable.

They had stood bravely for him against these adventurers who had penetrated into the ritual site deep in this cave.

True, it was greed and not loyalty that had motivated them, but his life was saved just the same.

He had a quest, a mission.

A crucial quest, bestowed upon him from the distant pitch-black beyond, by the gods of chaos themselves.

He trembled with joy each time he remembered their handout, their oracle.

It was a rare honor to receive a handout directly from the gods.

Those who were granted such things, if they were adventurers, became heroes. If they were aligned with the forces of chaos, they became legendary villains.

It led to death and glory, to honor and legend. To all these things, he held the key.

It was in a bizarre shape, like a twisted, empty talon stretching out to grasp something.

Now all he needed was living sacrifices.

However—he had by no means enough yet.

He would have to order the goblins to bring him more sacrifices. And if that was not enough...

Well, adventurers had a special love of money and women. They could be brought from order to chaos easily.

What a simple thing it was to brutally, cruelly overrun those made foolish by festivity when one was guided from within...

They would cross the defensive walls, tear down the decorations, slaughter those who fled in panic, rape, pillage.

And then he would make his offering.

The black-skinned dark elf smiled broadly thinking of it.

CHAPTER 6

SEVEN POWERS

The canary chirped against the pouring rain.

It sang a melody from its cage, and the droplets pelting the window formed the accompaniment.

Cow Girl sat by the window. She touched the fogged glass with a fingertip and exhaled.

She leaned on her arms. The dress she still wore was all that was left of her festival morning.

She could feel the cool air on her cheeks. A faint smile appeared, and she murmured, "I wonder where your master is now. What he's doing."

There was no reply. The bird just continued to twitter tunefully.

The bird he had brought home that summer now lived with them on the farm.

When she had asked, "Is it a gift for me?" he had replied, "Not really." He could be strange sometimes.

Strange. For him, that included going to a festival, or going on a date.

"..."

Maybe he's not coming back.

She buried her face in her arms as the thought crossed her mind.

She didn't want to see herself reflected in the window. She couldn't stand to.

Her right hand clenched. It still bore the ring—really just a toy—that he'd given her.

She'd been quite content with it when they were together. But now that they were apart, it was not nearly enough.

More, more, more.

More of what?

"Have I always been this selfish…?"

She could hear the throaty rumble of thunder in the distance.

Old stories told that such sounds were the voices of dragons, but she didn't know whether it was true.

Thankfully, she had yet to meet a dragon. And hopefully she never would.

Rumble, rumble. The thunder was getting closer. Thunder…?

Cow Girl realized the sound had stopped just near her.

That wasn't thunder. So what…?

She lifted her head, confused. She could see herself in the glass. She looked terrible. And past her reflection…

A grimy steel helmet, drenched with rain.

"Wha?! Oh… Wha?!"

She sat up in a rush, her mouth opening and closing.

What should she say? What could she say? Words and emotions whirled around her head and heart.

She couldn't quite manage *Welcome back* or *Are you all right?*

"Wh-what are you doing out in the rain like that? You'll catch a cold!"

That was the greeting she settled on as she pulled the window open with a bang.

"Sorry. The light was on, so I thought you were awake."

Compared to her disheveled state, he was so composed it made her angry.

"Something's come up."

"Something like…?"

"I'll be back in the morning," he said calmly, and then after a moment's thought, added, "I would like stew for breakfast."

"Uh—"

He would be back. He was going out of his way to tell her he would be back. And that he wanted to eat her cooking.

This man… Oh, this man!

"…Stew? In the morning?"

Warmth spread through her chest, and a smile lit up her face.

I'm such a light touch!

"I'm counting on you," he said.

All she could muster in response was, "Gosh, I'm hopeless" before she continued to say, "If you end up oversleeping because you catch a cold, I'll be angry. So make sure you're up on time."

"All right."

"…Mm."

Cow Girl nodded.

He never lied.

The "something" he was dealing with could only be one thing.

That's why she didn't ask anything else.

Their day of celebration was over. Things were back to normal. Another regular day.

Despite all she was feeling, this was not the day for showing her emotions.

"Well, then…o-okay."

There was only one thing she could say to him.

"Do your best!"

"I will."

And with that he took one step, then two, away from the window with the usual careless ferocity in his gait.

"Don't go outside," he said. "Stay with your uncle."

She watched him go until he vanished into the dark.

Rumble, rumble. The sound came again and grew more distant along with him.

Cow Girl saw what it was, and she chuckled to herself as she closed the window.

"Your master does the strangest things sometimes."

She poked the cage with a finger, causing it to sway gently. The canary chirped its objection.

But for once she paid it no mind.

Half of her was pouting in anger, the other half almost floating with excitement.

She had a sense this was not the time for these feelings—but she also wanted to go straight to bed and fall asleep still holding them to her heart.

Her dreams would give her time enough to enjoy them.

"But still…"

She took off the dress, folding it carefully so it wouldn't get wrinkled, then slid her voluptuous form into bed.

He obviously had something in mind.

"…Why in the world was he rolling those barrels along?"

§

The rain fell harder and harder as the wind grew biting.

The night was deep now, so inky black that it was hardly possible to see past one's nose.

This was a true storm.

"Ho, Beard-cutter!" Near the building that rose up out of the dark, Dwarf Shaman was calling. "I lit the furnace!"

"Did you?" Goblin Slayer stopped his rolling barrels, now at their journey's end, and nodded. The building—a small brick structure on the outskirts of the farm—had a chimney, but so far no smoke rose from it. "How does it look?"

"It was awfully damp. But nothing a little magic couldn't deal with."

Dwarf Shaman stroked his beard and smirked. Many of his special skills revolved around the earth, but dwarves and fire were also natural friends. It was simple enough for him to summon a Fire Salamander to ignite the sodden firewood.

"The direction of the wind seems good for now." High Elf Archer grabbed a spider crawling past and coaxed some silk from it, using it to restring her yew-wood bow.

All elf equipment was made from things found in nature. They might not have magic to control the spirits of the world, but from the day they were born, elves lived in true harmony with all things. Apparently, they felt that other races were simply oblivious, but…

It remained that there was no people in the world more suited to being rangers than the elves.

She flapped her distinctive long ears and said, "The storm is going to be right on top of us. But for now, we're upwind. Nature's on our side."

"All right. What about the goblins?"

"They're getting close. We don't have much time."

"I see. Let's hurry." Goblin Slayer nodded, then turned to Dwarf Shaman. "If you have spells to spare, try to intensify the wind. Just for good measure."

"Wind is the province of elves. Though I suppose I can find a bit of a gust, here…"

"Please do."

Dwarf Shaman responded to Goblin Slayer's request by pulling a fan out of his bag.

He opened it with a snap and began to sweep at the air, chanting in a strange, high-pitched voice.

"O sylphs, thou windy maidens fair, grant to me your kiss most rare—bless our ship with breezes fair."

Amid the howling of the storm, a softer current began to tickle their cheeks.

It was a simple spell for calling the wind, of the kind a mage might use when putting on a show for pocket change.

"That's about as strong as she gets," Dwarf Shaman said. "Don't know how much good it will do you."

"Can't you dwarves do anything right?" High Elf Archer chortled, drawing a barbed look from the shaman.

"I don't care. This is enough." With his back to the summoned wind, Goblin Slayer began checking all his preparations.

"How are your Dragontooth Warriors coming?"

"Everything is prepared."

Lizard Priest pointed to the small fangs scattered on the ground, then made his strange hands-together gesture.

"O horns and claws of our father, Iguanodon, thy four limbs, become two legs to walk upon the earth."

As his prayer resounded, the fangs grew, bubbling and rising.

Finally, two lizardman skeletons stood before them—Dragontooth Warriors.

Lizard Priest rested his Swordclaw on his shoulder and made an appreciative noise.

"Unfortunately, this represents the extent of my spells. Perhaps I could borrow something in the way of weapons for them?"

"No matter," Goblin Slayer said, righting the barrel at his feet. "I rent the shed over there. Use any of the weapons inside."

"Thank you. I shall appropriate one or two of them."

Lizard Priest curled his tail, and he and his skeletons lumbered away to the outbuilding.

As he took his leave, Goblin Slayer turned another barrel upright.

There were three barrels in all. They were almost as large as he was tall.

They also appeared to be quite heavy, packed with something inside. As he stood the barrel up, it landed with a spray of mud. It put dark spatters on Priestess's vestments, but she didn't seem to mind.

"Goblin Slayer, sir, aren't you cold?"

"If anyone is cold, I think it would be you."

Her thin garments were soaked through with rain, clinging tightly to her slim form. Priestess showed just a hint of embarrassment at the skin that was barely visible through the fabric, but she shook her head.

"No, I'm fine. This is nothing. Sometimes we perform our ablutions in ice-cold water."

"…You have miracles still, yes?"

"Yes, sir, no problem."

Priestess smiled bravely.

Her garments were, in fact, intended for battle, and the Earth Mother would hardly discriminate against a stain from the soil.

To dirty her pure white clothing in the aid of another would make her that much more beautiful.

She clutched her flail and nodded.

"I've had a chance to rest since I used Silence earlier. I can manage two more."

"Very well."

Goblin Slayer used the hilt of his sword to pry open the lid of one of the barrels.

It came off with a *screech*, and a raw stench mingled with the smell of the rain.

"Ugh," High Elf Archer said, scrunching up her face, but Priestess immediately reached into the barrel.

"We're out of time. I'll help!"

"Thanks. Please do."

"Sure thing!"

"Stuff them all in there. Every last one."

"Got it!"

She had pulled out a fish that had begun to rot in the sun.

She filled her arms with them, headed over to the furnace, and shoved them inside.

The searing hot flame was roaring now. They had not prepared it as merely a way to dry off from the rain.

As Goblin Slayer watched her, Dwarf Shaman elbowed him in the ribs. "Got to let the girl warm herself," he said knowingly.

"Erk." This came from High Elf Archer. "So what about me? I'm drenched!"

"Yes, yes, Miss Two Millennia. I thought the elves see rain as a blessing from heaven."

"Elves don't like being cold, either!"

And they were arguing again. It was their usual friendly banter.

Lizard Priest, who had returned from arming his Dragontooth Warriors with hoes and sickles, rolled his eyes merrily.

"And what exactly are you planning, milord Goblin Slayer?" His tone suggested this was what interested him most.

Goblin Slayer answered as he prepared his own equipment, making sure his shield was cinched down.

"It should be obvious. A basic goblin-slaying tactic."

He straightened his helmet and pulled the dagger he had stolen from a goblin out of a sheath at his hip.

He took a dirty rag from his pouch, carefully cleaning the blade.

He returned it to its sheath, then chose another blade with his right hand.

His dirty leather armor, his worthless-looking helmet, his sword that was neither long nor short, and the round shield on his arm.

With his unchanging appearance, in his unchanging tone, he declared simply:

"We're going to smoke them out."

Goblins were approaching—twenty or thirty, perhaps.

The smokehouse belched thick, black fumes into the storm.

§

For the goblins, this stormy night was a gift from above.

Night was their friend, and the dark their ally. The very thunder was their war drum.

Dark Elf, positioned behind them as their warlord, shared their sentiments.

He wore a grimy leather vest under an overcoat swollen and heavy with rain. A thin sword rested at his hip.

His skin may have been the color of pitch, his ears pointed like spikes, his hair silver—but he might still have passed for an adventurer. A good-hearted dark elf could come along once in a blue moon.

The weapon that he clutched, though, dispelled any question.

It was a twisted thing with an intricate pattern carved into it. At a glance, it rather resembled a candlestick.

Who could have wrought such a thing? Even now, it stretched out its fingers as if to grasp something.

And if all this were not enough, it glowed with the light of life, pulsating.

No partisan of order would wish to hold such an object.

"GOBOR!"

"GROBR!!"

"Mm. I care not. Continue the advance—trample them, bring them low!"

Dark Elf nodded placidly as one of his adorably stupid goblins gave a report.

The creatures made excellent foot soldiers but were eminently unsuited for anything else.

Of course, with simple weapons and armor and a position on the frontlines, they were more than enough to overrun the agents of order.

"You say there appear to be adventurers ahead? Dear fool. Quaking at shadows."

This was one of the cities where adventurers gathered. It was certainly possible some might be there. That was why he had deliberately arrived on the night after a festival.

"But…shall it go well for me…?"

Who was he to doubt the handout from the gods of chaos?

With the cursed object I hold, I shall summon the ancient Hecatoncheir, the hundred-handed giant.

Hecatoncheir, foremost among the fearsome giants found in the book of monsters that many believed the gods of chaos held. A creature created to do battle when the gods first began making the pieces for their war games.

He had heard how, with the power of its countless arms, it had struck down the gods of order.

Ah, Hecatoncheir! Hecatoncheir! Dark Elf veritably trembled with excitement.

His actions would make more certain the coming day of victory for the forces of chaos.

Ever since he had received his handout, he had spared no effort.

And yet somehow…he couldn't escape the sense that there was a flaw in his plan.

But why should he feel that way? For what cause?

Was it that communications with his squads to the east, west, and north had been mysteriously cut off?

Was it that the disgruntled adventurer he had hired to cause confusion in town seemed to have entirely neglected his job?

Or was it that all the women he had ordered his goblins to kidnap as living sacrifices had been stolen away from him?

Could it have been a mistake that this cursed object even came to him…?

"…No!" He bellowed as loud as he could, as if to banish his self-doubt. "The die is cast. Now there is nothing but to move forward!"

He had just thirty goblins with him under his personal command. But they were merely decoys.

So were the goblins approaching from the other directions. All simply to cloud the eyes of the adventurers.

The true mission was literally in his hands.

So long as he held this accursed thing, seat of Hecatoncheir's power, there was nothing to fear.

He would bide his time. Each hour, each second, wasting nothing.

He would offer up the dice. Seeking one more person, one more drop of blood.

Until Hecatoncheir awakened.

"Hrk...!"

Then it happened.

His senses, as sharp as any elf's, picked up something amiss.

A smell.

A stench, in fact, one that pierced his eyes and nose. Something rotting... No... The smell of the sea?

The rain and wind wiped out all sound, and now they carried a black mist that blotted out what little light there was.

It came on the wind, blanketing over his battlefield.

"A smokescreen? No... Poison gas?!"

He immediately covered his mouth, but unfortunately, his goblins were not so smart. The smoke enveloped them, and they began to scream and cry.

"C-curse you! You call yourselves adventurers, yet this is what you do to your foes...?!"

Dark Elf noticed his agitation rising, unable to restrain an angry snort.

This was hardly a tactic that the allies of law and order would employ.

But it was also not all that was in store.

Skeleton warriors emerged from the cloud, pale white against the black smoke, and laid into the goblins.

§

"You said you didn't set any traps, Beard-cutter!"

"I didn't."

Goblin Slayer spoke as they watched the goblins fall like wheat to a scythe.

"I did not say I had no plan."

"Oi."

"There is always a way. Often many."

"Oi."

The Dragontooth Warriors were truly terrible to behold on the battlefield.

They were only bones, lacking eyes, noses, and any need to breathe. The rotting fish smog had no ill effect on them.

The goblins were hacking and coughing in the cloud, swinging their weapons blindly. How easily the fossilized warriors overpowered them. One swing of a sickle severed a head. With a strike of the hoe, an arm went careening. The smell of blood and the reek of the goblins' own bodies joined the stench of fish in the air.

Perhaps hell smelled this way.

"You're not kidding," High Elf Archer said, scrunching up her face and covering her mouth and nose with a cloth. "You always have something up your sleeve for times like these, Orcbolg."

That was what made him the leader of their party.

High Elf Archer may have had more experience (or so she fancied), and Lizard Priest was perhaps a calmer head.

But when it came to sheer number of unorthodox strategies…

"But you can't use it on our adventure, all right? I'll get angry if you do."

"Not this one, either?"

"Of course not."

"I see."

Priestess giggled at his dejected response.

"Are you that disappointed?"

"When outnumbered by the enemy, it's an effective way to slow the vanguard," Goblin Slayer explained neutrally, then nodded with a grunt. "They search and investigate and become more anxious. They doubt what will come next. It's sleight of hand."

"I'm not sure those are really the same thing…"

No sooner had she said this than Priestess looked up at the battlefield as if she had sensed something. Her eyes went wide.

"Oh…!"

She trembled mightily as she called out, then leaped in front of the rest of the party.

Before anyone could stop her, she raised first her flail, and then her voice.

"O Earth Mother, abounding in mercy, by the power of the land grant safety to we who are weak!"

She implored the gods for a miracle. The all-compassionate Earth Mother bestowed her with an invisible barrier, centered around the staff she held in the air.

At that instant, the words of an ancient tongue rang out across the battlefield.

"Omnis...nodos...libero!" I unbind all that is bound!

An exploding light blinded them. A sheath of whiteness cut through the dark rain and enveloped everything.

It pierced the battlefield, cleared away the smoke, and shattered the Dragontooth Warriors. The skeletal soldiers collapsed like sacks of bricks.

The light pulsed across the battlefield again, catching several goblins and turning them to dust—

"Hrr...rrr..."

—until, with a crash, it slammed against the invisible barrier and vanished.

The rain whipped into a whirlwind, now with yet another strange smell intermingled with it.

Priestess reeled drunkenly, unable to completely absorb the spiritual shock of such an impact.

Goblin Slayer used his shielded left hand to hold her and keep her upright.

"I... I'm sorry..."

"Are you hurt?"

"N-no, my b-body is fine..." The blood had drained from her face, and she bit her lip regretfully. "But I... I only have one miracle left now..."

"No." Goblin Slayer shook his head. "It's enough."

The dark clouds that had covered the battlefield had been burned away.

They would not have long before the goblins recovered from their confusion.

The Dragontooth Warriors didn't last as long as I'd hoped.

Goblin Slayer quickly revised his plans. He had intended to move in only after the Warriors had reduced the goblin numbers a bit.

He did have one idea—not exactly a trump card, but something he had prepared in case they were facing something other than goblins.

But the farm was to their backs. They had to kill all their enemies here. Not one could be left alive.

Just as usual.

"What do you think?" he asked.

"That's got to be a Disintegrate spell," Dwarf Shaman said, stroking his beard as he dug in his bag of catalysts. "That's an ill thing to face, but chances are they can't do it more than once."

"It is strange, though," Lizard Priest said from where he crouched for cover in the undergrowth, watching the field alertly. "Would a spell-caster of such power normally split up his goblins?"

"Could he have some other aim?" Goblin Slayer muttered.

Dark clouds whirled above their heads. The elements lashed at them without mercy.

Goblin Slayer had a bad feeling. The same feeling he got when a goblin was sneaking up on him from behind.

"We have no way to buy ourselves time."

"There is an old proverb, 'A trap tripped is a trap no more.'" Lizard Priest swished his tail. "I think our best chance lies in a frontal assault, forcing his hand. You?"

"I agree," Goblin Slayer said shortly, then turned his helmet toward Priestess.

She wiped the sweat and mud and rain from her face and met his gaze.

His helmet was similarly soaked from the deluge, stained with mud and gore, and the expression within it was inscrutable.

"You're crucial. I'm counting on you."

But she could feel his gaze on her. She blinked.

It was more than enough to shore up the faith in her heart.

He—Goblin Slayer—this helplessly unusual person—

He was counting on her. He'd said so.

"...Yes, sir!"

"All right. Everyone, you know the plan. It's just as I told you earlier."

Goblin Slayer took up his sword, readied his shield, and stepped forward.

Lizard Priest lined up beside him, his Swordclaw at the ready, his tail raised.

In the rear, High Elf Archer set an arrow to her bow, drawing back the string.

Dwarf Shaman held catalysts in both hands as he began to chant.

And Priestess held tightly to her holy flail, offering a prayer to the gods in heaven.

"Let's go."

And so the battle was joined.

§

The first casualty was one trying to crawl away from the smoke screen.

The goblin cocked his head, sensing someone was approaching, and shortly after he no longer had a head to cock.

"GROORB?!"

Goblin Slayer stepped on the skull as he pressed forward, crushing it.

He swept the creature behind him with the shield on his left arm and pierced the throat of another that jumped at him.

"Two."

The fresh corpse fell back as he let go of his sword. He kicked it, striking out with the hand ax he had taken from its belt.

He cut the creature stumbling behind him at the base of its neck, claiming its life.

"Three."

He flung the ax casually into the goblin horde before collecting a short spear from his latest victim, and then pushed on without a glance back.

"This is the way. Let's go."

"Understood!" Lizard Priest responded smartly, bounding along, his tail curled.

He swung the White Fang like a broadsword, cutting down several enemies at a slash.

"Behold! Fearsome naga, my forefathers, behold! We revel in this night!"

"GOROROR?!"

Raindrops danced, blood flowed, and flesh flew. Yells and screams resonated in the air.

Goblins were born cowards. It was part of why they were so cunning.

Loath to die themselves, they used their companions as shields. Enraged at the resulting deaths of their allies, they swarmed together to overwhelm the foe.

And because their enemies had done them this grievous injustice, any and all torture was justified.

Look! The enemy is only two. Some have fallen, yes, but numbers are still on our side.

And amid the rain and the lingering vestiges of that awful stink—
Do you smell that?

A girl. An elf. A woman.

There is nothing to be concerned about. Do it.

"GOBBRO!!"

"GROBB!!"

It took only moments for the goblins' confusion to turn first to anger, then to greed.

Some took up their multifarious weapons and endeavored to halt Goblin Slayer's onslaught, and some brought out spears and sought to surround and kill Lizard Priest in his whirlwind of violence.

The more intelligent among them fled these terrible opponents and broke formation to escape.

But Goblin Slayer and his party were well aware that some were likely to try this.

"Pazuzu, Locust King, Son of the Sun, bring trembling and fear, on the wind you come!"

The goblins trembled at a sound like a high whistle on the wind.

And then they saw the source of the strange, howling rumble—a black wave rolling across the earth, straight at them. A storm of pitch.

It was a vast swarm of bugs, ready to overwhelm and destroy.

"GORRBGGOOG?!?!"

"GORGO?!"

The goblins tried desperately to sweep the biting creatures off their skin, unaware that it was only an illusion.

Fear was the most primal emotion in the world, and terribly effective at controlling the goblins. They fled screaming and gnashing their teeth.

They routed, dropping their weapons and running as fast as their legs would carry them in every direction.

As if they would get far.

"Gnomes! Undines! Make for me the finest cushion you will see!"

The goblins were ensnared.

The earth held their feet fast, and they flopped to the ground one by one. Sticky mud bubbled up around them.

"GORBO?!"

"GBORBB?!"

They struggled and fought but discovered they couldn't get up.

Lizard Priest made his way relentlessly around the summoned swamp, doing his deadly work.

Claw, claw, fang, tail. He danced among the goblins, sweeping them away with every limb.

"Ho! Forefathers of mine, who are part of my very being! Accept this rampage!"

The lizardmen came from the swamps. This mud was no hindrance.

Lizard Priest carved through the goblins, then raised his great head and howled.

"Onward, milord Goblin Slayer!"

"Right," Goblin Slayer said, coming up beside him. He carried some specially prepared leather.

He used his spear to stab one of the fallen creatures through the back. That was one. He took the monster's sword and threw it. Two.

He advanced with his shield up, knocking down several more near one of the bodies. He braced himself against the cadaver, pulling a sword out of it. Three.

He used that sword to split the skull of a goblin that tried to block his progress. Four. He dropped the blunted weapon, kicking a body aside and taking its club.

Coolly and precisely, seeking the greatest effect for the least effort, he cut a swath through the enemy force.

"Gods, Beard-cutter. He surely can handle himself." On the far side of the field, Dwarf Shaman laughed with a hunting horn in one hand and some clay in the other. That man defied belief. "Of course, without me here, things might not have gone so well…"

"*Make a swamp*," Goblin Slayer had told him. "*Don't let them get away.*"

Dwarf Shaman had had just the thing.

Fear, then Snare. The effects would only be amplified by the fact that they were outdoors.

Two large-scale spells. Admittedly, he was blowing through his catalysts, but…

"Look alive, Long-Ears, you're up next."

He gave her a hearty smack on the shoulder, and she flicked her ears at him in displeasure.

"Don't hit me. You'll throw off my aim."

"Don't be silly. A horde this big, it doesn't matter where you shoot, you'll hit something."

"You dwarves, never serious about anything… Those hits still only come after aiming."

She inhaled quietly, then exhaled from her nostrils. To an elf, shooting was like breathing.

Her fingers worked the string rhythmically, sending her arrows soaring through the rain. In this world, the gods alone could match an elf for sheer volume when it came to shooting. And High Elf Archer was, well, a high elf, the heir of a bloodline that stretched back to the age of the gods.

And indeed, her targets were goblins mired in the muck.

Despite her protests, she could have hit them without aiming. But she was too dedicated for that.

After all, Orcbolg had agreed to go on an adventure with her! She wouldn't let that opportunity slip away. She couldn't.

"Adventurers always see their quests through to the end!"

And her rain of bud-tipped arrows joined the rain that fell from the sky.

Goblin Slayer himself shot like a missile across the field, not a moment's hesitation in his step. This was not chance, but what needed to happen.

He had one aim—to reach the leader far behind enemy lines.

All the more reason…

"G—Grr!"

Dark Elf ground his teeth.

His thirty-goblin shield had been broken, the enemy was near at hand, and he had no time to focus on his chanting.

He thought of rallying his goblins, but he knew they would not come.

The one thing he could rely on was this. Dark Elf pulled his sword from its sheath.

"You damnable human!"

He struck, his blade a flash of silver light.

Goblin Slayer met it with his upraised shield. This was why he carried it. Its usefulness as a bludgeon was only secondary.

He immediately replied with a sweeping strike from the club he grasped in his right hand. He aimed for the head, hoping to shatter the skull or the spine.

But dark elves grasped motion as well as their forest brethren. In other words, far better than any human.

There was a spray of mud as the elf leaped backward, unperturbed by the swampy ground and not intimidated by the fearsome illusion.

Goblin Slayer's club connected with nothing but air.

"Hrmph. To think that one equipped to see through *my* plans should live in this town…"

"…You don't seem to be a goblin."

Goblin Slayer and Dark Elf now stood some distance apart. The mud softly sounded *slosh, slosh* as they shuffled to find an advantageous position.

Dark Elf's sword was clearly a better weapon than the adventurer's club.

Fully aware of this, the elf took the time to interrogate his opponent.

"Who or what are you?"

"…"

"I had heard that some in this town had reached the rank of Silver… But I cannot imagine such an experienced adventurer would stoop to using a goblin's club."

"Are you their leader?"

Goblin Slayer replied with his own question. Indifferently. Just as always.

"Indeed I am," Dark Elf returned, feeling a touch annoyed. His chest puffed out, and the corners of his mouth turned up slightly. "I am the apostle of anarchy, recipient of a handout from the very gods of chaos themselves!" He bore a sword in his right hand, a magical item in his left. Dark Elf kept a low stance as he exclaimed, "And my goblin army approaches from every direction! The next life will soon welcome you and your—"

"I don't know what you are. And I don't care." Goblin Slayer interrupted the elf's proclamation. "…That goblin lord was more trouble than you."

"____"

There was a pause as Dark Elf processed what had been said.

"Wh—why, you insolent…!"

His agile toes took a refined, complicated geometrical step.

From this unusual stance, his blade came like a flash.

The barely detectable glow was the proof of its magic latency. It was a magic sword. Not particularly unusual.

Goblin Slayer drew up his shield to block the blow. The strike ran along the surface of the shield, curving up and over it.

No—

"Hrggh!"

Goblin Slayer grunted.

The thin blade warped, piercing through his chain mail through a seam in his shoulder armor.

Blood seeped out on his left side. Dark Elf didn't simply have the better weapon, but was experienced in using it.

"Hah! You're slow, human!"

His skill should not have come as a surprise. After all, his level was high enough that he could even use Disintegrate.

Elves and dark elves had fundamentally different physicalities from humans.

Humans were not really naturally endowed in any exceptional way, which made it difficult for them to gain the upper hand over an agile dark elf. Let alone one like this, who had tens or hundreds or thousands more years of experience. Confronted with Dark Elf's eyes and hands and skills, just-passable equipment was as good as no equipment.

"I see. As their leader, you have no need to hold back."

Not that it mattered to Goblin Slayer, of course.

The hit wasn't critical. It didn't hurt enough to impede his use of the shoulder. And it wasn't poisoned.

He evaluated his own wound with his usual calm detachment, then elected to continue the fight.

"Still eager for more, are you, you dirty little worm?"

"..."

"Very well. See for yourself if *we* are less than a goblin!"

Dark Elf, who seemed to have jumped to some unwarranted conclusion, thrust the artifact in his left hand into the air.

"O lord of this great limb, prince of the hurricane! Set the winds blowing! Summon the storm! Grant me power!"

Something changed at that moment. An uncanny crackling sound came from Dark Elf's body. It twisted and swelled. Then, one after another, they burst from his back.

Arms.

Deformed and bizarre, bones connected in the wrong places, bulging with muscles.

Five of them in all—seven, including the arms he had been born with.

"...Hrm."

"Heh, heh-heh, heh. I see you cannot even speak, you accursed adventurer!"

The grasping appendages, like a spider's or crab's, were visible even from across the battlefield.

He was no longer truly a dark elf. His eyes were wild and bloodshot, his voice high, straining against the limits of all his senses and abilities.

©Noboru Kannatuki

He barely made a sound as he leaned in with his massive weight and dived at Goblin Slayer.

In the next instant, a geyser of mud shot from the earth, accompanied by a thump.

"What in the world is that?!" High Elf Archer shouted as she let off an arrow, catching an encroaching goblin through the eye. "Did that dark elf just grow arms from his back?!"

"Can't be! Ridiculous!" Dwarf Shaman already had his ax out and was putting it to good use against the goblins.

The work of the Dragontooth Warriors and the two frontline fighters had reduced the enemy numbers significantly. As long as the party could hold its battle line, they had a strong chance at victory.

"Blast! Whatever he's done, it seems to be some kind of magic. And it doesn't look like anything we want to get mixed up in!"

"Oh, I don't think we've anything to fear." That was the third member of the party. Lizard Priest, his tail curled up, sounded more confident than usual. "It's just a bit of instantaneous bodily transformation. Milord Goblin Slayer has everything well in hand."

That left them free to concentrate on their role. With a howl, Lizard Priest leaped anew at the goblins.

§

It was fair to say Goblin Slayer was holding his own against an enemy who could attack seven times at once.

He blocked an attack from the left with his shield, then struck out with his club. He rolled away from blows that came from every direction, then rose to one knee.

A fist came pounding down from over his head. This time he dove forward, straight toward Dark Elf.

"…!"

Goblin Slayer swept his dagger in upward, but Dark Elf's agility allowed him to dodge.

The creature's arms allowed him to nearly fly over the mud.

"What's wrong, human? You'll have to get closer if you want to use that blade of yours!"

Now that the enemy had widened the space between them, Goblin Slayer had no choice but to advance.

Dark Elf waited without so much as a wobble, despite the five massive arms growing from his back. The sight of him standing there, his balance unaffected by the new limbs, was most disturbing.

"Well, the bigger they are, the better targets they make!"

True, Goblin Slayer was at a disadvantage one-on-one. But didn't that simply mean he needed some friends?

High Elf Archer had just finished off some goblins nearby. Now she dropped to one knee and readied her bow.

She pulled an arrow from her quiver, nocked it into her bow, drew back, and released it in a single flowing motion.

Her aim was dead-on. The bud-tipped arrow slipped between the raindrops, struck Dark Elf in the forehead—

"......!"

—almost. The instant before it landed, a vast white hand suddenly appeared and snatched the arrow from the air.

It was like a whirlwind, like a pillar of stone. A hand swollen and bulging and twisted.

The translucent limb snapped the arrow like the branch it was and vanished.

Dark Elf smirked and held the cursed artifact in his left hand aloft.

No one would lead from the front lines without some kind of protection.

"He can deflect arrows...?!" High Elf Archer wailed, shuddering in terror.

It was said that in the depths of time, a giant had fought in the war between the gods of order and chaos.

That accursed artifact was its arm—an object with the power to summon the giant. And Dark Elf was its owner.

"So—" Dwarf Shaman slapped his cheeks, grimacing. "—he's a summoner?!"

If he could truly summon a creature from the age of the gods, that meant he was as strong as a Bronze or Silver adventurer, or even...

His summoning methods were unorthodox, indeed, inhuman, but there was no denying the confidence he exuded. It was possible that for Dark Elf, he himself—let alone his goblins—was not the most important thing.

Behold the dark clouds that roiled overhead. Behold the storm that made to attack the town. The thunder. The wind. The rain.

What if all of these were but the harbingers of Hecatoncheir's return to earth?

"If he deflects arrows, are we to assume that all ranged weapons shall prove ineffective?"

"I don't know exactly, myself..."

Lizard Priest had just returned from decapitating the last goblin covered in mud.

High Elf Archer's answer was accompanied by an anxious flick of her ears. Still reeling from disbelief, she readied another arrow.

"...But when I was small, my grandpa told me that no matter how many arrows were loosed at that giant, it stopped them all."

If a human grandfather had told such a story, it might well have been dismissed as a tall tale. But this was an old elven veteran who had been alive during the battles of the mythical age.

And he had said arrows were useless.

"Gods," Dwarf Shaman said as he clicked his tongue. "Of all the times for an elf to find out what it means to fail." He didn't seem open to optimism.

He held up a finger, judging the distance to the mutated Dark Elf. The enemy was just within his range.

But Stone Blast carried too much risk of hitting Goblin Slayer. And even if it struck true, how much damage would it actually do to those monstrous arms...?

"Oho?"

Dark Elf's eyes had gone wide.

Goblin Slayer had tossed aside his club and drawn his sword. The strange-length sword was covered in a film of dirt, perhaps from fighting in the mud.

But Goblin Slayer took a deep stance and rotated his wrist once.

"Do you imagine a change of weapons will allow you to prevail against me?"

"No." Goblin Slayer steadied his breathing, pointed the tip of his sword at the enemy, and spoke in a low voice. "I imagine it'll let me kill you."

"Spare me your idiocy!"

As he bellowed, Dark Elf's arms stretched unnaturally, reaching out toward Goblin Slayer.

The human warrior dove forward, taking advantage of the slightest of gaps.

In his right hand, Dark Elf held that nimble sword. It was a good weapon, but its owner's reflexes made it truly dangerous.

"A suicidal charge? You'll never reach me."

Goblin Slayer just managed to deflect the whistling flash of silver with his shield.

The piece of round leather had already sustained several cuts and piercings and was reaching a point when it would no longer be of much use.

But Goblin Slayer paid this no mind, closing the distance with his sword at the ready.

Dark Elf jumped backward and prepared to thrust again. Goblin Slayer followed, reaching out with the tip of his blade.

The enemy's chest armor cracked ever so slightly with a ringing echo. But that was all.

"Ha-ha-ha-ha-ha-ha! It seems your trusty *arm* isn't strong enough!"

Goblin Slayer simply didn't have the power to strike the elf himself.

The enemy landed on the ground, splattering mud everywhere, and declared in triumph:

"I have taken your measure! You are no better than Ruby, the fifth rank. Or even Emerald, the sixth!"

"No," Goblin Slayer said, shaking his head. "Try Obsidian."

Goblin Slayer didn't have it in him. But…

"O Earth Mother, abounding in mercy, grant your sacred light to we who are lost in darkness!"

They heard a clear voice, raised in supplication to the gods.

On this night of all nights, for a prayer from one she had so recently blessed with her love, how could the Earth Mother fail to grant a miracle?

Holy Light exploded from Priestess's upheld flail.

Uttering a soundless scream, Dark Elf retreated when a light as bright as the sun pierced the storm.

His eyes, accustomed to the night and the darkened rain, burned as if exposed to daylight.

Priestess no longer needed words to communicate with Goblin Slayer.

The party would handle the goblins; Goblin Slayer would handle their leader. And...

You're crucial. I'm counting on you.

He had entrusted this role to her.

Of course she would follow the path he carved through the goblin army.

And now, with the light at his back, Goblin Slayer surged into the darkness.

Priestess stood behind him, covered in rain and mud and sweat, yet immaculate in her resolve, holding the light high.

Her beauty did not come from the light of the gods that bathed her, nor from the vestments she wore.

It came from the way she could carry her prayer to the very place of the gods in heaven on behalf of another.

Without a moment's doubt or hesitation. Though trembling and afraid, still she raised her flail.

"Goblin Slayer, sir!"

His sword worked, though he did not shout or bellow.

He raised the weapon, advanced, took aim, let it fall, and cut his foe. It was a completely normal, totally unremarkable attack.

"Hrr—gah!"

But an attack it was.

Dark Elf's chest armor shattered, gore spraying. It wasn't much. But the blow had struck home, and that was enough.

"Wh-why, y-youuuu—!"

He dropped his sword and pressed his hand to his chest, stumbling back.

He had feared no arrow, nor indeed any sword or magic spell. That blow had wounded his pride as a dark elf far more deeply than his body.

©Noboru Kannatuki

How could this ragtag party of busybodies have brought me so low?!

"I shall make you *wish* I had merely used the giant's power to obliter-ate this town!" Murder blazed in his eyes. As much as forest elves seek harmony, dark elves cherish pride and torment. "I will make you food for my goblins. And your elf and your little girl—I shall cut off their hands and feet, then leave them deep in the nest until they die…!"

Dark Elf assumed it was his own burgeoning fury that made it dif-ficult to get the words out.

He fell to one knee in a spatter of mud.

"Erg… Gah… Hrrr…?"

His face, the color of darkness, contorted with pain. The five arms on his back clawed at the mud, and he struggled to stand.

Was it the summoning that had sapped his strength so suddenly? Impossible. If anything, it had brought him *more* strength.

The injury, then—the wound?

—No.

"It's poisoned."

Goblin Slayer offered only those two words and tossed out an old rag from the pouch on his hip.

It held the darts that had been used against him and Guild Girl in the attack at the Guild Hall.

Goblin Slayer didn't know exactly what kind of poison was on them, but…

"Wh-why, you—! You—! *Youuu*—!"

…to use it on his enemy, it was enough to know that it was poison.

Blood seeped out from between Dark Elf's fingers and ran to the ground.

Rage flared in his eyes, and the rain streaked across his contorting lips.

He used the arms on his back, instead of the ones that trembled on his torso, to prop himself up.

Lightning flashed behind Dark Elf, highlighting his unsteady form, like a withering tree.

He panted, fighting against the poison coursing through him. He looked like one about to die, and yet more terrible than before.

"Omnis...!"

He bellowed out the words of true power, a last-ditch death spell if there ever was one.

"No...!" Priestess tried desperately to hold her flail up in quaking hands, her face pale and bloodless.

But the strain of connecting her soul to the very gods time and again had made her fingers unsteady.

"If he hits us, it's all over, but—his guard's down!"

High Elf Archer pulled three arrows from her quiver, launching them at him all at once, quicker than magic.

But with a gust of wind, the cloudlike hand swatted away the arrows as they zipped through the storm.

"Hecatoncheir's great power...!"

High Elf Archer ground her teeth and angrily pulled out another arrow. She refused to believe it was useless.

"Stone Blast is too imprecise! It's up to you to save the day, Long-Ears!"

"What do you think I'm trying to do?!"

The archer loosed shot after shot, but the arm swept each one from the sky.

"My own spells and those of our lady the priestess are exhausted. Meaning..."

"Nodos...!"

Charge in for a melee attack? No, at this distance neither they nor Goblin Slayer would be in time. Lizard Priest joined High Elf Archer in grinding his teeth.

Dark Elf's incantation continued clear and loud. Their time was nearly up.

So—the party's eyes turned to one man.

"Goblin Slayer...sir..."

"Arrow deflection?"

Covered in mud and poison and blood, that steel helmet tilted ever so slightly.

"He is able to deflect incoming arrows...is that right?"

Despite the storm raging around them, his gentle murmur could not fail to reach the high elf's ears.

"Deflect them, defend against them—you know!" She raised her voice to be heard over the wind. "What…? What did my grandpa call it…?" She chewed on her finely formed thumb, flicking her ears in annoyance. "I think he said… 'No metal pierceth my skin, the shaft of every arrow is caught by my hand.'"

"I see." *No metal pierceth the skin. The shaft of every arrow caught.* He muttered to himself. "Arrow deflection…"

All this he said without emotion, then finally nodded to acknowledge Priestess's call and took a step forward.

Before his eyes, the white light was already beginning to shine. The air hummed with building magical power.

As he took a second step, he put his longsword back in its sheath and turned his right shoulder lightly around.

"Libe…"

"I see."

Then the third step. At that instant, Dark Elf's left arm went flying.

Nobody—including Dark Elf himself—realized it had happened until blood began gushing from the stump.

The storm picked up the spurting blood and scattered it like rain. The noise of the arm landing in the bushes could be heard.

The strange, bent throwing knife had cut through the air, and then through Dark Elf's flesh and bone.

The windmill-shaped blade. Dark Elf had no way of knowing it was a Southern-style throwing knife.

"—?! Gaaahhh!!"

The throwing star trailed through the mist as the chant morphed into a hideous scream.

Dark Elf clutched at his mangled limb. Behind him, the arm waved like a blade of grass in the storm.

"This is considered a dagger."

There was nothing at all remarkable about Goblin Slayer's throw.

It was simply fast and precise.

Two arms danced in the night—that of Dark Elf, and the one his hand had been holding.

They landed pathetically in the muck, and Goblin Slayer stepped on them.

From beneath his boot, there was a sound reminiscent of rocks cracking.

He didn't know exactly what had happened, but it seemed the arm now deflected arrows no more than a goblin's arm did.

"N-no! My—my arm! Heca—toncheir's—arm—!"

An instant later an unerring arrow pierced Dark Elf's throat where he writhed on the ground.

There was a distant exhalation from High Elf Archer as she let the shot go. This was all she could do without some sort of cheat.

"My...sacrifices...not enough...sacrifices... And my goblins...no... use...at all..."

Dark Elf hacked up a stream of blood, then focused his scorching gaze on the encroaching enemies.

But the fire in his eyes was low, indistinct. His vision was blurry. He blinked quickly.

All he could see was an adventurer in the strangest equipment.

Grimy leather armor, a cheap-looking steel helmet, a sword of strange length, and a small round shield strapped to his arm. He was splattered with rain and mud, blood and earth. Even a novice adventurer would be in better shape.

And yet...

"Y-you... It was you..." Bile rose with the blood in Dark Elf's mouth. "In the water town... The hero who...thwarted...our ambitions...!"

He should have seen it sooner.

Their revenge on that accursed Sword Maiden, the Demon Lord's revival, and the ritual to summon a storm of chaos.

It was adventurers who had put an end to it all.

This man. This man was one of them, he was sure. Dark Elf glared at that steel helmet with thoughts as bloody as his lips.

"......No."

He answered dispassionately.

So many people supported him.

Helped him.

Guided him. It was thanks to all of them that he was here.

When he went back to town, there would be those whom—regardless of how they might feel about him—he called friend.

If he turned around, he would see those who fought with him as companions.

If he went home, there was someone waiting for him there.

Not minions. Not followers.

Nothing given to him by the gods, by fate, or by chance.

But by choices he had made, paths and paragraphs he chose of his own volition.

All the more reason he could call himself what he pleased.

Ah, but…

All the more reason.

"I'm…"

Without a flicker of hesitation, he declared himself.

"…Goblin Slayer."

That was some adventure! Plenty of twists, a few turns...

Too bad there were still some bad guys leftover after we broke up the plans of that Evil Sect or whatever it was.

And whoever that giant was they were trying to summon, that seemed pretty badass.

The archbishop and I were finally able to meet up via the ritual at the harvest festival—even if it was only in spirit form.

That girl's prayer reached all the way to the gods. Awesome, huh? Way over my head.

That guy started spinning right in front of our eyes until he got as big as a mountain!

The clouds he stirred up around him stretched out and turned into these nasty-looking arms.

He was like a centipede in human form—it kinda gave me the heebie-jeebies.

I mean, right now I don't have a body, just my spirit. Even though I somehow have all my usual equipment and weapons.

"It can be rather unsettling to float along, and then find yourself facing your enemy in spirit form."

Sheesh. For someone who's trained enough to be a master sword fighter, she's sure got boobs to spare.

Look at all that! As long as we're just spirits, maybe I could fill out a bit, too…

"…Why do I feel like you're watching me?"

"Envy. I know the feeling well."

Oh, shoot. I forgot everyone can see your emotions here.

Aw, well. That priestess is about my age, and she's no bigger than me.

Isn't this lady supposed to be super smart or wise or whatever? And she doesn't know a single way to get me any more size. It's almost funny.

"Sore loser."

"Aw, shaddup!"

Apparently, this is the astral plane or something. There's this kind of gentle, warm light everywhere. It's really lovely.

The light is people's thoughts. Their feelings. I guess it just goes to show how warm everyone in this little town is.

That ice treat I ate in town was really sweet. Even if I went without lemonade because I couldn't get a single ball in that frog's mouth.

The bacon was salty and delicious, and all the performers put on really neat shows.

And those lanterns! I didn't get to listen to the whole prayer, but for sure I want to come back next year.

That's why I've got to stop this big guy from getting out of here.

That's reason enough…but…

"Hey, doesn't 'Hecatoncheir' mean 'the hundred-handed one'? I'd swear this guy has at least a thousand!"

"It's a figure of speech."

"It's a dirty lie!"

I guess it's a little late to complain now, but isn't that cheating?!

The god who gave me that handout—are they trying to get me killed?

That thing's whipping up magic like there's no tomorrow!

"Oh, man… Even I can't crit *every* time…"

"Hey, you hear that? The girl who always gets a breakthrough is saying something."

"You know, it *is* possible to be too humble for your own good."

"Pipe down, you guys, I'm trying to be dramatic!"

I flourish my holy sword, a completely unique weapon to which my soul is bound.

I have no idea why, but that creature was wasting time trying to manifest itself on the physical plane.

My friends and I will keep the world safe. We'll keep everyone safe. We'll put the hurt on the bad guys and everything will be fine.

Time for everyone's favorite—the climactic face-off!

"Here we goooo! Heroes, have at you!"

Sun Burst!!

©Noboru Kannatuki

CHAPTER 7

CHERISH THE SIMPLE DAYS

The autumn sun is weaker than the one in summer, but in warmth it's similar to spring.

Sitting on the grass under a sky as blue as paint, it was easy to drift off.

Cow Girl heaved a great, lazy yawn and smiled at the man with her.

"Ahhh, this feels great."

"......Mrm."

"Oops, did I hurt you?"

"No," he said. "But I don't understand why you're doing this."

"Because I want to?" She brushed aside his black hair with one hand, moving the little stick in her right hand in his ear. "Heh-heh! It's actually pretty fun, cleaning your ears."

"Is it?"

After that, he fell silent.

She took that as a good sign, enjoying the feeling of the weight on her knees.

A cool breeze blew out of town, over the hill where the daisies had been in bloom.

The sunlight was still warm, but the wind seemed to be growing colder.

A sweet aroma arrived on the breeze—fragrant olives.

Could the smell really have carried this far? she wondered.

The world seemed at ease.

He hadn't told her much, but…

The rain had stopped, the storm had passed, and everything was over.

Travelers on the way home frowned at the goblin corpses they found along the roads.

The low-ranking adventurers who had been dispatched shortly after dawn to clean up were probably none too happy, either.

But the one who had silently gone about digging holes and setting traps did not seem to pay it much mind.

The festival was over, and he had done what he had to do. That was all. And that meant…

"I have to go back to how I was, too…huh."

"…What's that?"

"N-nothing," she said, then brought her lips close to his ear and blew gently.

He shifted in surprise.

I knew this would be fun, she thought.

"Done. Flip over. I'll do the other side."

"…All right."

He obediently rolled over, like a giant puppy.

He was a bit too dangerous for a pet, though, and maybe not impressive enough for hunting.

A stray?

She stroked his hair at the thought.

"Not quite. You do have a home."

"What are you talking about?"

"Hmm, I wonder."

She chuckled meaninglessly and tugged on his ear.

"Stay still, now. I wouldn't want to get it too deep."

"That would be a problem."

"You could stand to be a little less serious, though."

She giggled. What did her laugh sound like to him, now that they were so close?

His voice was always slightly muffled by his helmet. Did hers sound the same to him?

As she mulled over these thoughts, he gave a grunt.

Noboru Kannatuki

"Sorry. Let's take a break."

"Huh?" Cow Girl blinked, but withdrew the ear pick. "Sure, but… What's up?"

"We have visitors."

He had heaved himself up. She followed his gaze and did indeed spot several people.

One was small, one slim, one short, and one towering.

"…Ahh." Even as she smiled in understanding, he was donning his helmet.

He lowered the visor, secured it, gathered his gear, and nodded. He was ready.

"You don't have to be embarrassed."

"I'm not embarrassed," he said as he stood. He surveyed the faces of his four companions, and then asked, "Goblins?"

"Yeah! And how! Not that I want anything to do with it, but…" High Elf Archer made a sound halfway between a snort and a sigh. "That receptionist girl pleaded with us, said nobody else would do it. So we didn't have any choice…"

"Let's go. Where is it? How large?" It took him no time at all to decide.

That was the answer he always gave. High Elf Archer rolled her eyes to the clouds, but Lizard Priest was used to this already.

"In the mountains. Evidently a rather sizable nest."

"All right. Equipment?"

"Oh! I already bought everything!" Priestess seemed simultaneously proud of herself and a bit embarrassed.

That explained the large-ish bag she was carrying. If they had to go into the mountains on foot rather than by carriage, they would need quite a range of items. And she was already enough of an adventurer to have thought ahead and obtained everything.

"Food and wine, I assume. And everything else we normally use?" asked Dwarf Shaman.

"Good." Goblin Slayer nodded. "Whatever else we need, we can get when we arrive. Was it a villager who filed the quest?"

"Indeed."

"Then they'll know the area. First thing when we get there, we study the terrain."

Cow Girl watched him prepare, one item at a time.

There was something irresistible about it, something so utterly reliable, and she felt a smile creep over her face.

She stood quietly from the grass. At the same moment, he turned his helmet toward her.

"Sorry. I'll be back."

"Sure. Don't worry about it. You're the only one who can do it, right?"

"...Yes."

Then he spoke up again, as if something had just occurred to him.

"The fragrant olives."

"Yeah?"

"I researched them, but I don't think they fit me."

"Oh, no?" Cow Girl cocked her head, the wind picking up her hair. "I think I'd have to disagree..."

"Would you?"

"Sure."

"I see."

And with that he fell silent and left on his adventure—no, his goblin hunt.

He would beat them. He would beat them and come home.

Cow Girl understood perfectly that this was how he would spend his days.

And she would spend hers waiting for him. Just as she always did—now that the festival was over.

She watched him go, smiling, then turned back to the farm with a whisper. *Now, then.*

The wind gusted from far away, carrying once more the scent of the olives.

Those flowers represented four things: purity, humility, true love... and first love.

I think it fits perfectly.

Her murmur, like the fragrance of flowers, was borne away by the wind.

Autumn had deepened, and the footfalls of winter approached.

AFTERWORD

Thank you, thank you. Kumo Kagyu here. I hope you enjoyed volume 3.

That means this is also my third afterword, but I'm still not used to writing them.

So, as ever, I'll start with my thanks.

First of all, I am so grateful to have made it to three books. It's all because of my readers, my editors, the bookstore people, and so many others. Thank you, thank you.

Thank you, as always, to everyone who encouraged me while I was writing on the web, as well as the site admin.

All my gaming friends, thanks again. I'm sorry for that incident where I mistook you for one of the zombies and blew off your head with a shotgun.

To my creative friends, I always find your advice extremely helpful. Thank you.

Mr. Noboru Kannatuki, thank you for providing another volume of wonderful illustrations. I'm sorry I don't have anything more productive to say than "Wow! That's amazing!" every time I get your pictures.

My gratitude goes out to all of you, all the time.

*   *   *

The first collected volume of Mr. Kurose's manga version of this series is coming out at about the same time as this book.

It's a comic full of goblins, whom Goblin Slayer slays. Wow! It's amazing!

Thank you for doing such constantly high-quality work. I'm sorry I don't have anything more productive to say than "Yeah! That's it! Do it! Finish him off!" every time I get your chapters.

I hope you'll continue working with a writer like me.

In this story, Goblin Slayer slayed all the goblins who showed up.

Maybe we'll do something different for the next volume. I'm thinking of a collection of short stories about what other people get up to while he's off slaying goblins.

And maybe Spearman and Heavy Warrior sub in a weirdo instead of their scout, and he guides them up a tower. Do the three of them get along or not? Well, that's how human relationships are. I think.

And then there's the drama CD… The drama CD? The drama CD! Hard to believe, isn't it?

I'm thinking it's going to be an adventure involving Priestess and High Elf Archer. I hope you'll enjoy it.

To the actors and staff, I look forward to working with you.

Gosh. Geez, I mean, I can't help thinking about what an incredible thing this has become. A year ago, this wasn't even my wildest dream.

I mean, really, we have no idea what life has in store for us.

It's brought home to me just how important it is to get yourself out there and do things.

And I'm going to do my best on everything coming up. I hope you'll join me.